Tiddley Trail Stories

With a Foreword by Reva Leah Stern

"If you like your coffee black and bitter, your stories on the weird and wild side with more twists and turns than a Canada's Wonderland roller coaster, this collection of short stories by Bala Menon is right up your dark and sinister alley. Nothing is as it seems. Nothing."

- Michael Joll, short story writer and novelist

"I have known Bala for over 15 years and wonder how such a gentle, friendly person can come up with such dark, devious, macabre and morbid story lines that keep you on the edge of your seat, waiting for twisted, disturbing and unexpected endings. His imagination is incredible and you can always detect a touch of humor mixed in with the twists and turns of his tales. His brilliant story telling will keep you engaged and wanting for more. If you like unusual stories, this book is for you; it makes for great bedtime reading."

- Konrad Brinck, story-teller and author of the acclaimed memoir 'It's Just Me!' and the travelogue 'Travelations'

Tiddley Trail Stories

Bala Menon

TAMARIND TREE
TORONTO

Library and Archives Canada Cataloguing in Publication

Title: Tiddley trail stories / Bala Menon.
Names: Menon, Bala, 1953- author.
Identifiers: Canadiana 2024048844X | ISBN 9781989242100 (softcover)
Subjects: LCGFT: Short stories.
Classification: LCC PS8626.E569 T53 2024 | DDC C813/.6—dc23

This collection of short stories is a work of fiction and solely for the reader's entertainment. All the names, characters, businesses, agencies, places, events and incidents in this book are either the product of the author's imagination or used in a fictitious manner. Any resemblance to actual persons, living or dead, or actual events, places and/or institutions is purely coincidental.

Cover pic: Fantasy forest—Under licence from: (2017) DarkBird/Shutterstock.com.
Pic of man/werewolf: By SilviaP Design via Pixabay. Layout by Vijay Mohan.

To my trail-builders: My parents

Other Books

Spice & Kosher: Exotic Cuisine of the Cochin Jews
- *by Dr. Essie Sassoon, Bala Menon and Kenny Salem*

The 'Jewish Gandhi' of Cochin: A Biography of A. B. Salem
- *by Bala Menon and Dr. Essie Sassoon*

Rhapsody Lane: A Collection of Works by Flower City Writers
- Eds*: Bala Menon, Rena Graefner and Konrad Brinck*

Crazy Cove: A Romp with the Writers of Courtney Park
-Eds: *Mary Ellen Koroscil, Bala Menon and Sheila Tucke*r

Contents

Foreword

When asked to write the foreword for Bala Menon's latest creation, "Tiddley Trail Stories," I thought I would be in for a jolly, giddy ride amidst a variety of delightful fantasy tales. I hadn't as yet seen the manuscript, but the previous work I had seen of Bala's was always rife with colour and wit. Then, to my surprise and delight, what I eagerly devoured in his latest manuscript, page after page, were tales of dark humour, irony, karma, and vivid imagination. For me, those are the ingredients that make for a delicious read. His stories range in emotional temperature, from chucklingly naughty, to shiveringly shocking, to pleasantly vengeful.

At the end of each tale, his more virtuous characters are generally left with lessons to learn, while he often, hastily and boldly delivers the comeuppance his fiendishly dark characters aptly deserve.

None of his stories are predictable or passive. These unique and eerie tales keep the reader engaged and agog from the beginning to the end.

My colleague, Bala Menon is a charming, intelligent, soft spoken, kind, and generous man. On meeting him, initially, one might be more likely to expect his stories to be chronicles of adventurers, healers, or dreamers. So much the greater surprise to realize that inside his exceptionally creative mind is a limitless lava flow of boundless imagery, places, and people. His courage is inspiring, and his "pen" writes with unshackled originality.

His stories are not for the cowardly or the cringey; they are tales to delight the adventurous who thirst for the days of Rod Serling and Alfred Hitchcock, artists who dared to step outside the cultural template to make us shudder in awe, and completely love the experience.

I hope this collection of tales, cheekily named "Tiddley Trail Stories" will surprise, delight, and give you a shiver or two as you settle into your most comfortable seat and absorb yourself in the unique world of Bala Menon's imagination.

Here's a helpful hint: before you become captivated by Bala's stories, maybe turn your lights on, and close your blinds.

- Reva Leah Stern, writer, editor, director and designer

Reva has written original stage plays, and directed, produced, and/or designed over 100 plays and directed over 40 television series episodes. She is the author of "The Water Buffalo That Shed Her Girdle," and a mystery novel, "I Say My Name." Her latest mystery/thriller, "The Prescott Journals," has been optioned for the screen. Her next project is a collection of short stories, "The Strange Spectrum of Mysterious Mishaps."

It Was Only A Mug of Coffee

I am a connoisseur of coffee, especially the kind made with a mix of Arabica beans and the Robusta variety. All these years, I believed that the best beans were those grown in the Ethiopian highlands. Ahh, the aroma when it's being roasted and the flavour when you sip it are just otherworldly.

However, six months ago, my taste buds shot into the stratosphere when a research chemist at my family coffee plantation in the North Sumatran hill country poured out an experimental mug of what she called 'something special' for me to sip.

'Amazing' was just a word until then—but then this was it. "Amazing, mind-blowing, I am brain-drenched," I told Adiratna. "Have we done it? Have we created the ultimate coffee experience?"

She was beaming. "Yes, we have most of the formulae…four years of intense work. We have to tweak it a little to make it on a commercial scale."

"Commercial!" I exclaimed. "It will destroy the global coffee industry. Hah! We will be the Great Morning Disruptor. Ours will be an empire. We will rock, we will roast, we will rule!"

For some years now, Adiratna and her team have been toiling in our laboratories for over 10 hours a day in total secrecy. No member of the team knew what ingredients the others were working with. It was essential that everything be hush-hush. The coffee industry is competitive, with each estate protecting their blends with high-tech surveillance systems, security guards and dogs.

My family plantation produces specialty coffee for boutique

stores around Asia under the brand name of Panch-Karya. You must have seen our coffee, with lustrous gold and black packaging, in fine outlets. This new product, however, if handled well, will take us to an international level and way out of reach of any coffee company in the world.

"All of you will be getting shares in the company," I told Adiratna. "You will all become very wealthy. The sixty workers in the plantations as well." I paused for a minute, then rubbed my hands. "Who else in the company knows about this, Adiratna?"

"No one. You are the first one to know. You are in charge of the labs and all the equipment."

"What about my brother and my sisters?" I asked.

Adiratna shook her head. "No, they know nothing yet."

"And my mother?"

"I thought it would be nice if you tell her," she said.

"Yes, you are right. I'll give the family the good news at dinner tonight. They will be thrilled. I hope it won't be too much for them to digest."

I followed her into what we called 'The Cavern'—the main laboratory that I had designed with some help from a Swedish architectural firm. 'I am good, I am a Boy Wonder,' I told myself as I looked around the high-domed room which had no corners. The upper part of the walls were of white marble, and the bottom was clad in stainless steel. There were flasks and casks with liquids in various shades of brown; some ranged from maroon to pitch black. Rows of test tubes rested on the workbenches, along with two huge, gurgling pots of tempered glass, containing an orange-coloured fluid. A massive stainless steel cylinder hissed, while puffing out pure white smoke. The sweetish bouquet of coffee was all-pervading.

It was Thursday evening. I asked the three chemists working at their stations to go home. "Take a break…for three days. We are going to redesign the lab and create bigger cubicles for you."

I waited for them to remove their lab coats and shuffle out, waving as they left, and then turned to Adiratna. "Where's the formula?"

"There are random sequences in five of those stations," she pointed at a bank of computers at the far end of the room. "None of them are connected to each other. We have to assemble them to make it complete. I have the final ten per cent in my unit."

"That is great… There will be a lot of work to be done, as part of a big expansion program soon. You will have to take charge. Okay, now tell me about the process—as much as you know."

This was Adiratna's territory and the words tumbled out. "You know how we do the *gilling basah* or the wet hulling of the beans. We depulp it, but instead of drying it out, what Cahyono, our plant manager, did was to leave the moisture content locked in at 40 per cent. We removed the skin and were left with the green coffee beans. I tested it and found that it had low acidity and the brew was thicker."

In the highlands of North Sumatra, light and shadows interplay as the mist rises from the nearby Lake Toba and settles as dew on the coffee plants. Our workers pick the beans in the early morning before the dew disappears. What Adiratna and Cahyono did was mix these beans with those from a small, research plantation on the Ijen Plateau in the eastern part of Java, which is also part of my family estates.

So now you know why coffee is sometimes called java!

There were other steps—which Adiratna was not aware of—but structured by other chemists.

"So what about the final touch?" I was impatient.

"I found a number of new plants sprouting under some of the coffee shrubs." Her eyes sparkled. "I distilled the leaves and used some drops on a few selected samples."

"And then…?

"They were tobacco leaves… strange with some pale, pinkish nodules. I think it's some sort of fungus. I tested them; they are not poisonous. The composition is like the *Phallus indusiatus* mushrooms, found in our forests." She giggled. "The name is because of its bell-shaped cap, like a penis. I don't know how it reached our estate. But the molecules I scraped from the pink nodules merged easily into the core of our beans."

Adiratna said the secret was in the mixture's gassing, which let off a type of light green steam or mist into the vats with the beans.

I already knew that Bagaskoro, one of our chemists, was experimenting with cocoa beans, drying it out to a minimal moisture content of ten per cent and then spinning it in a small centrifuge along with the coffee beans. He did mention in a note that the molecular ensemble had a leathery structure, and the beans then gave off a faint fragrance of crushed ginger and sandalwood. Over the past six months, the lab had cultured the beans to perfection..

The only thing now left to do was to combine the formula fragments into a complete unit. My new coffee will neither age, nor lose its aroma and flavour. You will never feel the sour or bitter taste that coffee throws up as the shelf life advances, much like old men who become obdurate or women who turn into shrews. My coffee will stay virginal forever. Yes, forever. The oils in the beans will become fresher as the molecules collide and interact with each other.

Later, as part of an expansion program, my chemists can infuse this coffee with fragrant rose water, saffron, peppercorn, cinnamon, cloves or cardamon. The branding possibilities seem limitless, with exotic names for each new variant.

Exultant, I went for a long walk in the coffee estate, savouring the stillness of the late evening. Reclining later on a rocking chair inside a glass-roofed shed, I looked at the stars and inhaled the euphoric scent of the highlands. I thought of my father and grandparents, who created and developed these impressive properties on the Sumatran hillsides. I have trudged on the narrow paths, on which dried leaves crunched with delight under my feet, trekked along the craggy outcrops, clambered atop the rocks and ran when I felt like it. I said a silent prayer, thanking them for their bequest to us.

Four days ago, however, as the Hari Raya Lebaran (Eid) holidays began, I did something which I should not have done. It was downright, irrational behaviour.

Nobody in my family or the company knew that I had overriding power over all the servers and security systems. I knew I was dishonouring my family and breaching their trust as I slipped into the lab late at night. Copying the entire formula onto a flash drive, I encrypted it and wiped clean the hard drives in all the six computers used by my chemists. Nobody in the world can now ever know the secret of the soon-to-be sensational and stimulating 'anytime' brew. Not my siblings, not my mother. I must handle this momentous invention alone. Before the break of dawn the next day, without telling anyone, I snuck away from home.

After parking my SUV in the underground garage at Kuala Namu International Airport, I booked a ticket to the Soekarno-Hatta airport in Jakarta, with an onward connection to Toronto.

While on my flights and during transit, I arranged via my phone a series of meetings with selected members of the Coffee Board of Canada in Calgary after four days and the American Coffee Federation of the United States in New York two days later. Patenting and licensing the formula was important; that is the way to maximize earnings for years and, maybe, decades, to come.

At Toronto's Pearson International Airport, I rented a flashy sports car and decided to drive to Calgary. I had always wanted to enjoy the expansive scenery of Canada, a country about which I had read and heard a lot about, and had no time to waste with a hotel stay in the asphalt jungle that is Toronto. I found myself enthralled by the pink of the dawn peeping through the thick woods of Ontario, and the bright orange of the sunset in the prairie region in Manitoba, with two night halts at motels. I was in a dream-like state. My thoughts were on the billions of dollars that would be coming our way, and about building a new family home on a lush and enchanting island somewhere in the Pacific Ocean.

What would my mom and my siblings be doing now? They must be wondering where I went. I will wait until later in the week, after the money deals are finalized, to call them.

Anyway, here I was in a coffee shop in the seedier part of a small town in the country's midwest—somewhere in the province of Saskachewan—where I halted during the drive along the TransCanada Highway. The glass window and door panes of the store had Espresso, Cappuccino, English Toffee, Mocha and Macchiato, scribbled with big white paint. The interior decor of the place was hideous.

I sat at a corner table. There were a few customers, some seated at the tables, eating what looked like sandwiches. Three men, who had followed me inside, were standing by the cash counter. They were all staring at me.

Oh, my goodness! Did any of them see me park the car? They know I am a foreigner, with my South-East Asian features. I shouldn't have come inside this joint.

The waiter—a small, well-dressed man—placed a menu card, stained with ketchup, in front of me and asked, "Wanna something to chow down? Fried chicken?"

I had already eaten a roast beef sandwich, bought from a gas station's food outlet on the way; the time was around 4:00 in the evening and I was yearning for a coffee. I asked for a plain cafe latte and the man shuffled away. After about five minutes, he appeared and placed a mug in front of me.

The liquid looked brackish, but I took a sip. Never in my life had I tasted anything so noxious, so abrasive to the palate, so galling.

I don't know what came over me. I was in a state of emotional intoxication or indignation and just couldn't contain myself. I summoned the waiter, stood up as he approached and threw the coffee at him. "This is not coffee... It's a shitty, brown goo. You drink it," I said. I threw a five dollar bill on the table.

"'Yes, sir," his voice was soft as he wiped the coffee off his shirt front with a napkin. He didn't look at me.

Walking out of the cafe, I stepped into an alley which would take me to the main road where I'd parked my car. It had been raining and there were puddles of muddy water everywhere. The brown brick buildings around looked old and rundown. There were only a few pedestrians in sight, some walking with umbrellas over their heads. A group of youngsters lounged against the wall of a building near the cafe, smoking. The smell of marijuana was strong in the air.

I shouldn't have left my briefcase, with my travel documents and cash, on the seat of the car. Big mistake. What was I thinking?

I took out the flash drive from the inside pocket of my sport jacket, turned it around, felt its smoothness and whispered, "Wow, yes, I have this…Calgary, here I come, with a carafe of the finest coffee in the universe. It's time to smell and taste the real world."

Somebody yelled, "Hey, you," behind me. I turned around and there was the mousy waiter, crouched on the wet ground as if he was about to leap over something. He had unbuttoned his shirt—and bared his hairless chest. He had a snub-nosed gun in his right hand.

Petrified, I shouted, "Okay, guy, Okay... I am sorry about what happened in there..." I raised both my hands. "I am really sorry... I didn't mean it."

Some men came out from the cafe and formed a circle behind the waiter, who wasn't moving. I stood still for what seemed a long time—and then the waiter stood up. The young men, who were lounging against a wall near the building, were walking towards me. I swung around and ran.

The next moment, I pitched forward and went sprawling on the cracked and pot-holed road. Searing pain leaped through my spinal cord and into my brain. The drive flew out of my hand and bounced several meters down the road towards the gutter, with its runoff water rushing into a storm drain.

A hand was rummaging through my jacket and trouser pockets. I felt my wallet being taken and somebody pulled off the gold chain from my neck, and removed my bracelet and watch. A man yelled, "Take his phone."

"My flash drive... My formula." My voice was hoarse.

Something hard crashed on the back of my head.

A puddle turned into a delicate pink near my stomach, bubbling and expanding into coffee-coloured rings towards the alley edge.

"Ah, you are back in the world of the living," the doctor said. "You were in a sedative-induced coma for the past eight days. I am Dr. Sergio Lubash, your neurosurgeon. Do you remember anything?"

I blinked. A couple of nurses stood around the hospital bed, adjusting an intravenous line on my left hand. There is a tube running into my throat and another on the left side of my stomach. I am numb all over. I can't turn my head; a skull-fixation device is holding it in a tight grip. Two monitors are beeping. I can see their flickering green lights from the corner of my eyes and can hear them; they sound like musical notes on a synthesizer.

"You are in an ICU here at Saskatoon General," Dr. Lubash said. "There were two complex surgeries performed on you. This is my assistant, Dr. Misty Nayyar, who helped me in the operation theatre." He nodded towards a young woman in a medical gown and mask standing at the foot of the bed. "You are lucky to be alive. The paramedics said you had lost a lot of blood...They brought you here just in time. Can you hear me and understand?"

I blinked again.

"That's good. We don't know who you are...There was no identification on you. We didn't know whom to inform about your condition." The doctor paused. He scanned through some pages on a clipboard that he lifted from the base of the bed. "You were shot in the back and the bullet shattered three of your upper vertebrae, with extensive damage to the nerves. We had to fuse them together and so you will have to live with the kyphosis, that is the medical term for curvature of the spine—like a hunchback."

I was blinking rapidly and my tears welled up. A terrible feeling of sadness crushed me; as if I had lost something valuable. I just couldn't recollect what it was. Not my spine... Something other... Something like a bird that flew away from me... Gone.

"Lots of questions, yes? You will be okay, you will live," Dr. Lubash said. "Oh, and you will have to give a police statement tomorrow morning about how you landed in that area. Was it in a car? It's a known hot-spot of crime. Do you remember anything about the mugging? That's what the police admission report said."

Dr. Lubash shone a light into each of my eyes, and pressed his fingers on the side of my neck. He looked at one of the beeping monitors and then turned to one of the nurses. "Give him a vial of atropine. His heart rate needs to climb a little. Record it on the file and add some zolpidem to the IV. That will make him sleep for some more hours."

He patted me on the shoulder. "There will be some physio later. But there will be no more sports, no running, no trekking, no mountain climbing for you ever; your spine might just give way. I will be leaving in a few minutes... If you need anything, Dr. Nayyar will be here. Your throat will be scratchy for some days."

A nurse flipped a switch to raise my bed a little and said, "We will remove the feeding tube in the evening and you will be able to enjoy a plain meal of chicken broth."

Dr. Nayyar moved to my bedside. She waved the nurse away, leaned towards me and said, "Now, about that soup, yes. There are two other issues you must know about. There was a blow to the back of your head. The trauma impacted the gustatory cortex in the anterior insula and the frontal operculum of your brain. Here and here." She touched the back of her head and her forehead.

She spoke slowly, every word like a new blow on my head. "We performed some complex microsurgery... But the receptor channels for many taste sensations of the posterior and lateral sides of your tongue are damaged beyond repair. Most foods will taste sour or bitter. We hope it might get better as time goes by... Or maybe never."

Dr. Nayyar paused, as if to give me time to digest the information. My eyes were tearing up again as I blinked. A nurse handed the doctor a moist towelette, and she wiped my cheeks. She looked at Dr. Lubash, who nodded for her to continue.

"I am afraid the olfactory nerve in your temporal lobe was also affected—we call it neurotmesis—it has caused severe functional loss because of a pathway disconnection. You will smell things only in a faint way... Very, very faint."

The Bank Client

It was a blustery, but bright, Monday morning, during the snowy days of January 2021, when the COVID-19 pandemic was raging across the world. The Government of Canada had just rolled out the COVID-19 vaccination program across the country.

Death and illness were the dominant topics in all conversations. The economy was in a downward spiral, causing people to lose jobs, businesses to shutter, and ailing seniors to be put on ventilators without being able to see their loved ones. All this added to the general gloom. As a financial advisor at one of the top Canadian banks, I still had to answer questions from desperate clients on problems related to house purchases, down payments, mortgages, loan defaults, and other transactions. Plus, I had to be a good listener as well, with many clients often unloading their personal problems in my office. After the first lockdown, we received instructions to report to the office as usual.

That morning, I entered my office, hung my winter jacket and handbag on hooks near my office window, adjusted my mask, and sat down. I switched on my computer, took out my phone and sent a message to my husband, "Don't forget to take extra masks with you when you leave."

I also sent messages to my children. "Don't waste time listening to music or watching cartoons. Don't miss the online classes. Make sure to do your homework, and eat your lunch on time."

There was only light walk-in traffic at the bank when Henry Randall arrived unannounced and entered my office. I was adjusting frames on my desk—one with a picture of my husband playing soccer with my daughter, and another was a photo taken at a Muskoka resort of our small family of four, with our dog.

Henry was a small, round man and I have known him as a long-time client with some personal investments. The bank also held the mortgage of his family home.

"Oh, I wasn't expecting anyone. Did you book an appointment? There is nothing listed in my schedule."

"No, Ma'am, Mrs. Jones. Sorry, about that."

I got the distinct impression that he was a little drunk. He sounded distant and not the usual passive and deferential man that I thought he was. He pulled out the chair from under my table and sat across from me.

"I was in the area and I had to withdraw some cash." He pointed towards the tellers' counters and the lobby. "There are not many customers. So I thought I will come and talk to you."

I said, "It's a Monday, and we have to chart out our weekly plans. However, I can spare you thirty minutes."

He was staring at the photographs on my side desk. "You have a happy family, Ma'am," he said, pointing at one of them."I am envious... My two sons are all grown up and gone. And your dog in the picture, is it a Pomeranian? He is so cute."

"It's a she," I said. "Millie is two years old. Yes, she is cute."

Henry's face crumpled. "I am stuck alone with Loretta, you know, my wife. Can't go out because of this lockdown stuff... It's a very lonely life; it's miserable. I only have my liquor bottles for company. And, you know Loretta."

"Of course, I know Loretta; she is such a gentle, sweet woman."

Henry rolled his eyes and waved his hands around. "Mrs. Jones, Ma'am..." His voice dropped and I had to strain to catch his words. "I wish... I wish the COVID virus will come and take Loretta away. I am fed up with her... And she has asthma. So you see, COVID can easily do her in. I have heard that the virus affects the lungs and then the other organs, doesn't it?"

His words shocked me. "What are you saying, Mr. Randall? Stop this, and tell me how I can help you today. You had mentioned about some investments about six months ago."

The Randall family lived in a comfortable house in a community on the edge of Scarborough. Henry said his realtor had appraised it around one million and six hundred thousand dollars. "It's not bad, you know. I paid only three hundred and fifty thousand for it just eighteen years ago."

He opened a folder full of printed sheets and spread out his hands.

Look at his hands. They are too big for his size. I have heard of 'sausage fingers', but God, those giant fingers can go around any-one's throat. Ugh... I have always had this 'ugh' feeling when Henry Randall displayed his hands.

"I might need some advice soon on a new mortgage," his voice was soft. He was leaning forward, conspiratorial. "A lot of changes are happening in my life, you see." He looked around and then began fidgeting.

"Well...?" I nodded for him to continue.

"Now, you see, Ma'am, I don't like living in the city. I am a bricklayer, I am a road builder and I am a handyman. I want a house with a nice grove of fruit trees in the yard, and some land for a garden to grow some seasonal vegetables."

He took a deep breath, exhaled sharply, and shook his head. "I want chickens to run around the yard and I want to eat fresh eggs every day. Maybe raise some turkeys as well. I want to smell the mud and trudge around in slush after the rains and I want two or three terriers running after me all day."

He produced a faded black-and-white photograph from his folder and extended it to me. "That was Robin, my Jack Russell terrier, when I was twelve years old. He was my constant friend until I was twenty-six. He lived for fourteen years. I want more such companion dogs in my life."

He started shaking his head again. "I can't even bring a little dog into our home today. Loretta doesn't allow it. She says, 'There will be dander; the hair will stick to all my dresses; the house will smell like a kennel.' Just a spunky, little dog... That's all what I want," his voice softened.

"Well, why don't you sell this house and move?" I asked, knowing that he wanted me to ask that question.

"'You know my wife, Loretta, and you think she is sweet and doesn't talk a lot? But that's all she does at home. Talk, talk and more talk. Yak, yak, yak. You see, she doesn't want us to move. She says she is a city girl and Geez, I don't know why she keeps calling herself a girl. She is now fifty-five, and has three wobbling chins."

I tried hard not to smile.

Loretta is a jolly, round hulk of a woman, who towers above Henry and she has a lusty voice. An incongruous couple, a total mismatch. Wonder how these two ever got together.

Henry scratched his head and then began cracking his knuckles. His words came out non-stop, like an express train. "She wants lipstick, she wants coffee shops, she wants her shitty hair done, her shitty nails all polished. She says we are getting old and here in the city, we have TransHelp if we cannot drive one day. We have hospitals nearby and there are doctors and pharmacies and dentists in every strip mall. And we have physiotherapists to work on her back if she gets back aches and..."

I interrupted him. "Well, but that's what everyone wants today. The convenience of everything, the comfort, you know, and the accessibility to services you need."

He wasn't listening. He rambled on. "And then I tell her, 'Darling, you are talking about something ten to fifteen or even twenty years from now. And you don't have any backache.' I mean, she has never spoken about an aching back so far."

"Then she argues, 'What if I get backaches? And what if you have a toothache? And what if you slip on the ice during the winter and fall? Out in the country, we won't get immediate help.' She goes on and on and on, strident, unending and with an opinion on everything, blah, blah, blah… yak, yak, yak."

Henry was now all puffed up. He pulled up the mask that had slipped down from his nose. His eyes glinted, and he shifted in his chair. "What do I do with such a woman? She has no reasoning power. She has no brains. She is stupid and always talking of tomorrow. Tomorrow we will do this, tomorrow we will do that, next year we will do this and that and after three years we will…"

"What about your children? Where are they now and what are they doing?" I wanted to derail this conversation.

"Oh, who cares about them? They moved away. Both are in the U.S. One is in Ohio and the other in Alabama."

"But you could visit them, drive down or fly to wherever they are," I pressed on.

"No, no..no…They don't care for me, and I don't care for them. Both are good for nothing, and I don't know what they do. They don't call me and I don't call them, but I know Loretta keeps in touch with them. It's one big secret. She doesn't talk about it, though. I think they are conspiring to swindle me out of my money. Ah, but she is a brilliant actress… She pretends everything is fine between us, all hunky-dory, like all the high-class people say. She even tries to hold my hand when we go out."

"I don't believe a word of what you are saying. You are just imagining things," I said.

His voice was now like a whisper. He was fixated on Loretta. "Loretta tried to kill me one day, y'know. I am certain of it."

"What are you saying, Mr. Randall?"

"Yeah…We had gone to Pembroke five months ago, with some friends. And from there we rode on a gravel road… It's about twenty kilometers to the Barron Canyon. Have you been there? It's an amazing hike up—a loop of about two km. On the top of the hill, at the edge of the canyon, Loretta tried to push me. I felt her weight on me. There are no railings, only lots of loose stones and that drop—Can you imagine?… Deep down the jagged rock cliffs and into the Barron River… That would have been goodbye for me… Somehow, I regained my balance. And y'know what she said? 'Oh, my God, I am so sorry, Henry' and turned away, maybe to hide her disappointment."

"I don't believe it," I said. "Loretta is not that kind of person."

"Oh yes, she is…Believe me, she is." He wasn't listening to me. "I have heard that it's easy to get rid of somebody if you hit them with a car. That is not murder, it's just an accident, isn't it? Even if you are charged, it's just a mild sentence. Sometimes, I think I should run over her in our driveway or push her into oncoming traffic when we are on a sidewalk or somewhere." He started giggling. "But she is so fat, it will take some pushing."

I bolted up from my chair. It was time to stop this conversation. "Okay, Mr. Randall. I have another appointment in about five minutes. Why don't you come in next week and we can talk about your finances, mortgages and retirement plans, all right?"

"Will do that," he said. After staring at me for a few uncomfortable seconds, he pushed back his chair and stood up. "I will drop by another day. It feels good talking to you, Ma'am."

Funny man. He has always been so staid and aloof. And just look at the way he is talking today. I am sure he is drunk.

Reaching home, and after dinner, with my two children in their rooms, my husband and I were watching television when the news came on about a murder in the east end of the city.

I remembered Henry and his conversation. "You know, a strange thing happened this morning," I told my husband. "We have a client called Henry Randall and he had come to the bank this morning. It was funny because instead of talking about money matters, he kept talking about his wife and how bad she is and how he wanted her out of his life. Maybe even kill her."

"What? He said that? He used the word kill?"

"Something to that effect. I don't remember the exact words. I stopped him when he was going off on a more dangerous tangent, and then he left. I am wondering if I should report him to the branch manager or maybe tell the police. I mean, what should I do?"

My husband, Cameron, is a professor of engineering at a local community college. He can put two and two together, like mathematical equations. He always says I am an empath and people gravitate towards me to talk about their private demons.

"This is a problem, Shirley," Cameron said. "We don't know his state of mind, do we? What if the manager calls him and scolds him or if he then reports it to the police? That could aggravate the situation. He might even try to attack you... These things happen... If he has any psychopathic tendencies..."

"But we can't ignore or forget this kind of talk, can we?" I said. "My worry is what if he comes in again to the bank, or what if does something to his wife... And then, I could be called in as a witness or an accessory—if he says he spoke to me about it."

"There is a possibility about that. But I would put that ratio at around sixty/forty. If that equation changes, then we should act."

We pondered over the issue for about an hour. Then my husband said, "I think we should ignore it at the moment. Maybe he was just sounding off, just talking out loud. This COVID issue is creating a lot of personal tensions everywhere. If he comes to the bank again, tell him in that stern voice of yours to talk to a marriage counsellor or that you will have to escalate the issue to your superiors."

It was now April 2021. The government was now talking of rolling out second doses of the COVID-19 vaccine, and most companies had their employees working from home. My bank had, however, classified some of us as essential workers. As a result, I had to come into the office every day.

Again, on an early Monday morning, Henry Randall appeared in front of my desk without an appointment. I had forgotten all about him, and I thought maybe he wanted to talk about a new mortgage proposal or a new savings certificate. The air was still nippy outside, with a light rain, and I was not in a pleasant mood, because most of the staff were at home and there were few clients in the bank. Half the advisers' cubicles were empty and not lit up.

Henry stood in front of me, holding a drenched baseball cap, and said, "Ma'am, I must speak with you." His eyes were bloodshot. He pulled out the chair from under my table and sat down without waiting for my response. "You see, it's about Loretta, my wife, y'know."

I was rather flustered. "Why do you want to speak about Loretta, Mr. Randall? I cannot advise you on anything personal. You can talk to me about money issues, or joint accounts with Loretta. There is nothing else about Loretta that concerns me, right?"

He spread out his fat hands again with those massive sausage fingers. "I know, I know. But, you see, one of my fellow workers, Mike... Mike Doyle, he is also a close buddy of mine. We work on the same floor of the new building under construction on Weston Road. We lay bricks, you see, one on top of the other, and he was telling me that we can trust only three people in this world."

I frowned, but my mask hid my frustration. "What?" I asked.

"Mike says we must trust only our doctor, our lawyer, and our banker. And I like Mike a lot... He's very wise with such things. I don't have a lawyer, and I can't go to my doctor and talk openly. I don't have any disease right now. He might tell me to see one of those mind doctors, you know... Shrinks, the loonies. They hypnotize you and do many strange things."

He paused for effect. "So that leaves only you, Mrs. Jones. You are a fine banker and a great person."

"Thanks for that," I said. "But if it's about you and Loretta and your life together, I think it would be better if you both consult with a marriage counsellor. He or she can help resolve any issues between you. Or would you like to speak with my manager?"

He either didn't hear me or was pretending not to. He leaned over, picked up one of my ball-point pens from the desk and started turning it around, clicking away. "You know, I saw in a film how a man killed several people with just a pencil. Just think if it was a pen like this. I mean, it can go easily through the folds of fat around Loretta's neck." He snickered. "She wouldn't even feel it, would she?"

"Come on Mr. Randall, you shouldn't talk like that," I was getting scared of this conversation. I tried to pacify him. "Okay, okay, I think you should go home."

He was still not done. "The other night, it was around three or three-thirty in the morning and Loretta began howling. That was scary... Like a wolf, really howling in her sleep. I shook her hard to wake her up... That fat lump, that mountain of a woman. Just imagine, if the neighbours had heard her... They would have surely called the police. I mean, she was loud, just like an animal."

Henry put his head up and raised his hand to the ceiling. "Like an animal. She was in a daze. She said she saw somebody chasing her in the street, swinging a machete, and it was late in the evening. It was near the park where we sometimes used to go for a walk under the trees. She says 'It was a nightmare, Frank. And that person looked like you, Frank.'

"I then tell her, 'Loretta, my name is not Frank... Who the hell is Frank?' And then she mutters, 'I don't know any Frank'. She drinks some water, turns around and goes back to sleep."

He was fidgeting in his seat. "D'you know, Mrs. Jones, Ma'am, the strange thing...The strange thing is that I had a fleeting thought that morning of chasing her somewhere in the dark in the park near our home and chopping her down with a machete. We all fantasize about these things, don't we? But how on earth could she have had that nightmare? Any idea?"

I had heard enough. I got up from my chair and said, "We are done, Mr. Randall. I have no interest in listening to you any more. You should leave now or I will have to call our security officer."

"Sit down, Mrs. Jones," his tone was menacing, coming from deep down in his chest. I sat down.

"I wish, I sometimes wish that Loretta would tumble down the stairs in our home from the top step, roll down, you know, like thud, thud, thud, and break her neck. No whimper. No blood and no mess. Clean. And then I can just move to a small town in northern Ontario. I have seen a wonderful little piece of property that is just waiting for me."

I got up from my chair again. "Okay, Mr. Randall, please, I have another appointment." I looked at my watch. "In about six minutes. I think the client must be already waiting. Why don't you come in next week and we can discuss your plans for the countryside property?"

He seemed to have quietened down. "Yeah, I know, I know. Anyway, thank you Ma'am. I will send you all the documents you might need for us securing a new mortgage. If you can help with those, let me know how we should proceed. Thank you for hearing me out. I will contact you later, hopefully in the fall."

He left, bouncing out through the door, pulling down his mask to flash a big-toothed smile at me, followed by a wink.

COVID-19 marched on, claiming lives and destroying families but I stayed busy—working sometimes from home and sometimes visiting the office.

A year had passed by and days were soon becoming distant memories. It was April 2022. It was another Monday morning with little walk-in traffic at the bank. A secretary handed me a heavy brown envelope with my name written on it with a green marker and said that someone had dropped it into our mailbox.

The envelope was from Henry Randall and contained several documents related to a house nestled on six acres near Huntsville in the Muskoka Region. There were several colour photographs of the heavily wooded property taken from different angles, displaying a two-storey house with a white, wrap-around porch.

This is good. Everything must have worked out well for the Randall family, after all. I was worried about nothing.

"It's a very picturesque place and just as I imagined it to be. There are some great weeping willows which I love. I have selected three dogs as well, two three-year-old bull terriers and a Jack Russell puppy. I will create a poultry corner somewhere on the grounds later," Henry had written, in a neat cursive style, on a sheet of paper. "I want an appointment in early June to finalize the mortgage details."

November 2022. It was a crisp and cool day in the middle of fall. I had just entered my office and switched on the computer when one of the tellers popped her head round the door.

"Hey Shirley, there's a woman waiting to see you," she said. "She has no appointment, but if you have a little time, she would like to see you now."

"Okay," I replied. "I have nobody booked for another two hours this morning. Tell her to come in."

"Hi, Mrs. Jones." Loretta Randall was loud, her lusty voice echoing round the room. I barely recognized her. She must have lost over fifty pounds and she was wearing a swishy, stylish outfit and looked just great. A bright, yellow bomber jacket was over her shoulders, the sleeves hanging free. She pulled back the chair and sat across from me. "How have you been? I have been wanting to come and meet you, along with Henry, but you see... This COVID issue and with all the lockdowns to deal with. It's been such a long time. Henry did mention that he met with you last year a couple of times."

"Yes, I know. I didn't have an opportunity to speak with many clients face to face during the past year or more," I said. "It's nice to see you after such a long time. You look incredible, so svelte..."

"Oh yes, thank you. I had bariatric surgery done... Got my belly all stitched up... And I have shed around 80 lbs."

"It's an amazing transformation, Mrs. Randall," I said. "I wish I coud lose some weight... Anyway, let me first pull up your account and then you can tell me how I can help you today."

"I just came to talk about closing our accounts at this branch," Loretta said. She sounded a little sheepish and apologetic.

I saw on the computer screen that the Randalls had applied for a mortgage closure on their Scarborough home and got the discharge papers five months ago. They had also transferred about three hundred thousand dollars to one of our competitor banks—the residual money—after a real estate sale and purchase combo. I saw they had arranged everything through a mortgage broker.

They didn't even have the courtesy to inform me about it, after all these years of being with this branch. Anyway, that's how people do things nowadays. There's no such thing as loyalty any more.

"I am happy for you," I said. "It's wonderful that you decided about the house in the country. Mr. Randall had written to me about the property in Huntsville in April. He also had written about arranging an appointment, but then I didn't hear from him again. So you didn't have much of an argument with him about moving to the countryside, I see."

Loretta was wearing a black mask so I couldn't read her face. "Yes, yes, we were getting around to it. But there will be no country living for me, Mrs. Jones. I am adamant about that. You see, we all have our wants and ideas, but the universe decides, doesn't it? Or God or whatever... However, our Scarborough house has been sold, and we moved into a lovely two-bedroom condo on the Lakeshore waterfront. It's on the eighth floor."

The glitter on her eyelids sparkled. "In late April, about six months ago, on a Saturday morning, Henry tumbled down the stairs from the top step, rolled down, you know, like thud, thud, thud, and broke his neck. He did not whimper. He shed no blood. There was no mess. Everything was clean... And we received quite a pile of insurance money."

"Oh my God," I exclaimed. "I am so sorry to hear about this. Accept my condolences. He was such a sweet man to talk to."

"Don't you worry, Mrs. Jones. Henry is not dead. He broke his neck and part of his spine, so he is in a wheelchair—and he can't talk. A caregiver comes in every three days. For now, anyway."

"Oh dear," I said. "That is a big problem. You mean, he can't walk, he can't drive... He can't talk?"

"It doesn't matter anymore. He sits by the window most of the time, looking at the lake and buildings outside. I turn him around on some days to let him watch me put on purple eyelashes and dark pink lipstick. He hates me doing that, you know... And sometimes, I walk around in a black lacy bra and mauve or pink panties, and I ask him, 'Horny Henry, you can't fuck anymore, right!?'

She was now laughing aloud. "Don't look so shocked, Mrs. Jones... And it's great fun when I blow marijuana smoke on his face. He hates the idea of women smoking..."

Loretta stood up, and adjusted the collar of her jacket. "Thanks for everything, Mrs. Jones. Please close all our accounts here and transfer the funds into my personal account at the Wilmingham Credit Union in Oakville. You have all the necessary documents."

At the door, Loretta turned towards me and said, "There's only one thing that worries me. I don't know when Henry will decide to fall out of the window. He wants it kept unlatched, always. Anyway, Frank, my gym trainer, is waiting for me in the car. Bye, for now..."

In The Knickknack Shop

'My dear *Umma* and *Kajok* (Mom and Family)', Hana Mae Mun read the letter she received that morning from Canada. The 'From' address on the envelope was in Mississauga, Ontario. Seated in front of her, Hana Mae's two sons and a group of shirtless, tattooed men paid close attention to her words.

Her voice wavered for a moment as she read aloud: 'I am sorry that I left you all and came to this country. I wanted to get away from the lifestyle of our *Kajok*. I realize the mistake I made. I have lost all my money, and all that you gave me—after I took a loan to start a small business here. I am sorry I failed you, *Umma*. Don't think bad about me, please. I am all right now. I have fallen, but I will get up again, maybe in another world.'

Hana Mae took a deep breath and said, "Kang is in trouble. Our eldest son has written some more lines about his problem, but I will keep that to myself for now. This is how he has ended his letter: 'Don't let the *Da-Sut-byeol kkangpae* know about this. I don't want any revenge taken in my name. Please don't send anybody here. *Salanghaneun adeul* (Your loving son), Kang.'"

Hana Mae Mun, based in Mokp'o, was a senior member of *Da-Sut-byeol*—the Five Star Mob, a crime syndicate in the underbelly of the southwestern region of the Korean peninsula. She commanded a sizeable battalion of *kkhangpae* (gangsters). She looked up and ordered her second son Hoon, "Book me a ticket to Toronto... and I will travel alone. Kang needs me, and I have to right some wrongs."

The elderly woman, wearing dowdy blue trousers, a wrinkled

blue cotton shirt, and a light blue baseball cap, turned a heavy bauble around in her hand. It was a cheap glass object, painted orange with disorganized blue streaks running within it and disappearing into nothing.

"Don't touch it," a voice whispered near her ear. There were three or four other customers in the shop and the man didn't want them to hear him. "You are leaving finger marks all over it."

Hana Mae glared at him. "Who are you?"

"My name is John Reid. I'm the owner of this shop."

The store, which sold knickknacks and cheap copies of brand-name crystals and porcelain figurines, was located in a strip mall near the Eglinton Hospital in Mississauga. It was busy most of the time with relatives and friends of patients waiting for the hospital visiting hours to begin. It was early in the morning and some stores in the mall were just opening for business.

The woman moved to another shelf, this time picking a black and silver swan, in blown glass. The man was close behind her, crowding her, trying to turn her towards the exit.

"What does this cost?" Hana Mae asked, turning the glass paper-weight in her hands, her finger running along the stylized neck of the swan and along its sharp three-inch-long beak. It was comforting, she thought. It was like touching the cheeks of a little child.

"I told you, don't touch it, stupid woman," John Reid, who also doubled as the salesperson, said. "You can't afford it. I am busy, see. I have other people to attend to... And more decent people will be coming in soon. Don't leave smudges on it."

"My name is Hana Mae Mun. I am 71 years old and I am not stupid. I don't leave any finger marks. What does this cost?"

The woman's eyes blazed, like a flare-up in a gas fire, as she glared at the man. "Why did you steal this store from my son? Do you think his family in Mokp'o and Busan will forget the humiliation that you piled on him? Do you think we will ever forgive you?"

"What, what?" the man said. He looked flustered. "Who are you? Go away, go away..."

"This shop belonged to my son Kang, who put his life and soul into making it run. He spent a lot of the family money. You snatched his happiness, pulled out his insides, and ate his soul."

"Look here, you old hag, I don't know you and I don't know any Kang or Wang and I don't care. I bought this shop fair and square from an idiot who couldn't run it."

The man squinted, made a face and waved his fingers. "I have not dealt with any person of your kind, somebody who looks funny like you, from your part of the world, wherever that is…okay?" Spittle flew as he sputtered, "Who are you, gargoyle? I don't have to talk to you or explain anything to you, okay… Just get out now… You don't belong here. Ching, chong…"

Hana Mae rounded a shelf, taking slow and measured steps, as John Reid followed. 'Where do these bloody people come from? Bloody third world immigrants,' he mumbled. He was now trying to shoo her away. He prodded her with the middle finger of his right hand. "Come on, leave… Or I will call the security people."

"You engineered a fake auction," Hana Mae said, pointing a finger in Reid's face. "Your people run a pawn shop and you threatened my son. You sent people to his home to hound him for more money."

Reid took a step back and stared at her.

"My son had paid off the loan and double that in interest. But your people assaulted him. *Flectere si nequeo superos, Acheronta movebo*," she hissed. "If I cannot bend the will of Heaven, I shall move Hell. That was Virgil speaking. Latin."

"You are mad… I am telling you again. I don't know who your son is… I don't know any pawn shop… I have had this store for the past three years," Reid said. "Why are you walking around with my art piece? Keep that back on the shelf. You cannot afford it. Leave… Please leave the store. We don't want you here and we are very busy now. Go take a shower, woman. Just go away. I don't want to know any of your kind. What nonsense is this…?"

Hana Mae moved to a corner of the store, behind a couple of shelves. The entrance to the store and the main aisles were now out of her sight. She placed the swan on a shelf and pulled out a wallet bulging with dollar bills from her shoulder bag. Reid's eyes also bulged. The wallet seemed to heave, breathing and pounding like his heart. His tone softened. He wrung his hands and put on a mocking East Asian accent. "You like that wonderful piece? Take it, the jewel costs only one hundred dollars. It's from Switzerland. Want a lookee around the shop! See, this lucky Buddha will look good in your home. Big, lucky Buddha, heh, heh. Look around... You want something for your grandkiddies...Hey Madam..."

The woman's eyes were now half closed. "Come closer, come closer and then take flight," she murmured. "Your time has come and no more a burden on this earth will you be..."

"What, what?" Reid said as he peered into her eyes, drawing closer to her. His eyes grew bigger and rounder, and he saw the universe swirling in Hana Mae's eyes. Planets, stars, and galaxies racing away from each other.

"I am old. No one will blame me. No one will see me. And your decayed mouth is an outlet for evil. Enjoy my wrath, Mr. Creed!"

"Creed? Mr. Creed? What are you..?"

"I am a little girl! Look." She tapped her forehead. *"Mihi vindictam ego retribuam.* Latin. Vengeance is mine, I will repay."

Hana Mae's hands flashed like a Hapkido martial artist. The wallet went into her bag and she picked up the swan, balancing it in her right hand. She swung around, her left hand squeezed Reid's windpipe and the glass beak of the heavy figurine plunged into his left eye like a spoon into yogurt. She pulled it out, swung again and the beak punctured and slashed his left carotid artery open. Hana Mae waited a few seconds and then let him go. Reid fell back onto a glass shelf, his scream coming out like a little squeal. Ceramic plates and cups clattered onto the floor and smashed into shapeless fragments as blood sprayed across the floor.

Four storefronts away was a shop selling costume jewellery and faux leather handbags. A young salesman was extolling the stitching quality and style of a purse to a well-dressed woman.

"Okay, I like it, I will buy it," she said, running her fingers around the corners of the purse. "Looks good, like one of those expensive and branded European bags."

"Yeah, they are great imitations and everybody loves the designer features. Do you want to have a look around the store?...I can discount some items...We have a stock clearance coming soon..."

"I will come in tomorrow with my husband. I want to look at some of your jewellery as well. Those zircon stones in that necklace over there look like real diamonds," she said, taking out a credit card to pay for the purse. "How long have you had this store? Lots of interesting things here..."

"Oh, I am not the owner of this shop. I am just the salesperson. Sean Creed, who is the owner, bought the store with all its contents at an auction about three months ago." He pointed to a corner of the store. "Mr. Creed is in the cubicle over there."

The salesperson printed out the receipt for the bag and handed it to the woman. He said, "The previous owner was an Asian man—his name was Kang. I worked for him a couple of months. I heard he had taken a big loan and couldn't pay it off. You know how some moneylenders are. They are real vultures... I shouldn't talk like this, you know, but it was Mr. Creed's family that forced the auction. So he is the new owner."

"Kang tried to commit suicide," he said in a hushed tone. "He drank some poison and barely survived. He had invested all his money into this shop. Very nice guy... Always smiling. He has nobody here... He was estranged from his family, who is somewhere in Korea. He always talked about his mother, though."

"What's that commotion outside?" the woman asked as emergency vehicles with flashing lights and blaring sirens raced in and screeched to a halt. Police officers and paramedics swarmed the strip mall, putting up yellow tapes around the perimeter. Loudspeakers called out for all shoppers to leave the stores.

Around the corner, nobody saw Hana Mae Mun leave through a side door of a knickknack store and nobody remembered seeing her in the mall. Security cameras had clear images of many people, but not the face of an elderly woman with a cap limping into the shop.

A dejected Hana Mae sat sipping roasted barley tea, in a motel room, a block away from the Eglinton Hospital. Her youngest son Yeong had packed several sachets of the tea in her baggage along with shrimp crackers and rice cakes, so that she didn't have to forego her favourite snacks in a foreign land. She was watching a news reader on TV saying that a shop owner had been stabbed to death in a strip mall near the hospital. The victim was identified as one John Reid and police were still scouring the area.

Hana Mae looked at the letter in her hand, written by her son Kang, who was in hospital on life-support and unlikely to survive.

I will go see him later, if he is still alive. How could I mistake Jon Lideu for Syeon Keulideu? I read it all wrong. Kang's writing is terrible...Creed, not Reid. Sean not John. But Reid deserved to die— jug-eul jagyeog-iissda. *He insulted me, he called me dirty...*

The next morning, Hana Mae was in the office of the Kongguksu Restaurant on Hurontario Street. "You know me?" Hana Mae asked the manager, who was standing before her and trembling with fear.

"Yes, godmother, *eung, daemonim*. I know and I respect you."

Hana Mae drank a couple of spoonfuls of the soup made with egg noodles in a broth of shellfish and dried anchovies, placed before her. "This is good. Let your eatery prosper."

"What can I do for you, godmother? Do you want soldiers? I am your servant." The manager bowed, bending low from his waist.

"I need a small dagger, you know, a *Dan Geom*, and a throwing knife, a *Dando*. Also, three sticks of gelignite. I don't want you or anyone from our country living here to get involved. Get me those things by the evening and leave them at the back door of the restaurant. You have not seen me or heard of me, ever." Hana Mae stood up, pulled her jacket close to her, patted the manager on his shoulder and walked out.

I don't think it's possible to get close to Creed, any time in the mall, to use the dagger. Let me find out where he lives... I will have to settle for the Dando to get deep into his heart, during the evening hours when the twilight dissolves into the night on a quiet street. And then burn down his home and wipe out his family. I can't return to Mokp'o, without wreaking blood revenge.

Just Go Away, Mommy!

"Are you old, Grammy?" my youngest granddaughter Rachel asked me four years ago. She was just five.

I laughed. "No, I am only forty-two."

"No, no, no, you are older," said Rachel, shaking her head.

She danced around me as I rocked in my chair on the deck of our backyard garden. The purple hydrangea was in full bloom in the corners, and the white, climbing roses were thick on the far fence.

"I know Grammy. You are old... And you have a lot of money, lots and lots and lots…"

"Okay, I am fifty-two, my dear child."

"No, no, you are old... I know you are seventy-four and you have lots and lots of money."

I stopped rocking. She stood in front of me, this lovely, precocious child, her face close to mine, her breath smelling of milk and cookies.

"When are you going to die, Grammy?" She was now staring at me, and pressing her hands on my chest. She wouldn't let go.

I looked at her, gulped, blinked and gulped again. The evening sun no longer felt warm. The trees fell into a brooding silence as a coyote's howl echoed in the ravine. Rachel's frock, with its bright yellow flowers, now appeared as a black gown. I rubbed my eyes.

"I heard Mommy and Daddy say you should die soon. They are in the kitchen, and they said they need your money. They said you are a money bag. When are you going to die, Grammy?" She giggled. "Where do you hide all your money, Grammy?"

It seems like yesterday that little Rachel, daughter of my youngest son Derek, spoke like this and bounced away into the house, leaving me alone to ponder about life and living and our transient ties with our loved ones.

Four winters have come and gone since Rachel's foretelling of my fate. Over the years, I felt a chasm widening in my relationship with my children. I have sensed their greed, their grasping nature, but didn't have the heart to throw them out of my house... Because a mother's love knows no boundaries. I lived in my house as a stranger, with visits to the seniors' recreation centre and meeting with my friends as the only joyful moments of my life.

There are only a few days to go before my children will kill me. It's Sunday today and they are planning the execution for this coming Friday. They calculate it will be two full days before the world knows that I am dead and gone! Natural cause of death, of course. Complications because of old age.

I have heard them mumble, whispering in the corners and behind the pillars in the basement. 'It's time for Mom to go. Her days are done,' I heard Derek telling his wife Cheryl some days ago. 'We can't bear this burden and why should we spend money to send her to a long-term care facility?'

Derek was a late arrival at our home and was born some eight years after our daughter, Janet. We showered all our love on him, the baby of the family, a gifted child who enriched our lives with his pranks and non-stop prattle. My husband, Jonathan and I always said we should opt to stay with Derek in our old age.

'She's a real burden around our necks,' said Cheryl. 'And it's disgusting how she spoils the sheets on some days. Ugh…'

Anguish has turned my heart into stone. Banished in the basement of my home a few months ago, my life today is a story of emotional abuse, stories of the kind I have read in newspapers, about cases going on in various courts.

I can hear all of them upstairs, living life as I did in my younger years with my husband and these same children of mine. I can hear my grandchildren laughing and screaming and running around, but they don't come to me anymore or come down to check on me to see if I'm all right or if I needed anything.

'No going into the basement...That isn't okay,' I hear Cheryl admonish her children. 'Don't disturb Grammy. She is very sick.'

The children have outgrown the awareness and love for me they once had. As for Rachel, I haven't seen her even once in the past two years. Her elder brother, Ryan runs down often to pick up a ball that has rolled down the stairs or to pick up a toy from a cupboard in the corner. He doesn't look at me. I have tried to call out to him, to tell him I am not sick; it was just a stroke and that I will get better, but he just laughs and runs away.

Now, back to the murder plan.

"Derek, this has been going on for over a year now. My God, she is seventy-eight, and look what a mess her life is. This misery has to end," my daughter Janet, who was visiting, muttered from the corner of the room, after standing by the bedside and staring at me for some time. She didn't hold my hand or say 'Mom'.

"And what about her estate? You know, we have placed a deposit for that downtown restaurant we want to run and another installment is due in a month's time. What's the use of that four million dollars of investments in Mom's name? And the cash accounts? It's all sitting idle in the bank. When can we use them? We need it. She doesn't."

"Yes," nodded Derek. "And there's the cottage near Tobermory, the farm in Milton, and there's this house."

"Remember what the doctor said—that her heart is fine and she could live for another ten or 12 years or more," chirped Cheryl. She sounded unhappy. "And with some physio and other therapies, she could walk a little and start speaking again. That's not good, is it?"

My son and daughter and their offspring think I can't hear or see them. It's obvious they have written me off; I am a wretched, shapeless lump on the bed. They now talk aloud about my condition in front of me, standing around me by the bedside or sitting on chairs near the stairs. A stroke about a year ago left me paralyzed, but I am aware of everything. My hearing is now sharper than ever and some of my memories are coming back into focus, although I can't speak right; and I can't get out of bed without help.

They are not my family anymore. Our connection broke in its totality after doctors said there was some strange activity in my brain. They said something about protein deposits, a mild atrophy natural to aging and an aneurism that caused the stroke and other things which I didn't understand. Shortly after that, they confined me to the basement, ceasing all hospital visits and prohibiting any visitors.

Until around six months ago, many of my children's friends would call, often dressed in face masks and gowns over their summer clothes. They'd stand there, gawking as I lay on the bed. The ghouls.

Although my friends came to see me, I couldn't talk or move in those early days because I was paralyzed. My thoughts came out incoherent, a jumble of words that sounded something like "plsst-mlssk-shish-blish-ploo". Now, there are no visitors. My son has told everybody that his ailing mother should not be disturbed. Even my closest friend, Mary Jane, was likely told that her visit would distress me and trigger a severe depression. It's all lies. They want me to be forgotten by my friends and the world, I know that. I'm desperate to see Mary Jane.

Ahh... back to the method of execution. Yes, I have heard that too! My loving son Derek is going to carry me off the bed, early on Thursday morning, and take me to the spa-like washroom, which my husband Jonathan built.

Oh, I recall those days when we used to shower together, standing under the rain-like faucets and feel the thrill of multiple water jets tingling our skin, or just sitting in the tub together sipping some wine from glasses on the sideboards. The bathroom walls are light green with unique leaf-like patterns, and the recessed lighting creates a nice tropical ambience. Jonathan used to love the woods, to hike in the hills, to cycle through the trails and he always wanted me along on his outings. How I wish he was still here with me...

'Andrea, we have brought up our children well, don't you think?' he would ask whenever we reached a lookout point and gazed at the thousands of trees in the valley or ravines below.

I would always nod and say, "Yes, we did."

Those days were enchanted. I was living in a world of magic. When Derek's children came along, a son ten years ago and a daughter two years later, it was as if heaven had opened up in full glory to us. Our family was complete with Janet and her two sons also visiting every weekend. The squealing laughter of the grandchildren, boating on the lakes, visiting the beaches, long weekends at our country cottage, going to the movies, shopping in the malls; our lifestyle was remarkable. It was our cosy, loving world—until the walls of my world collapsed around me and muddled up my life.

Why did you have to leave me so early, Jonathan? It's now five years... Why did you ride your mountain bike near that grotto when you knew there were loose stones on the cliff? What do I do, what can I do, I'm so alone... And scared...

In recent days, there has been an uptick in their whispering behind the beams and the corners of my basement prison.

That Derek, he is a sly one. He once brought in a lawyer friend of his to get me to sign off on some papers so that he and Janet could control my money. "She can't take any decisions by herself. She needs help," said Derek.

"We want to keep her comfortable. She always wanted to live in the basement after our dad passed away," added Janet. "And we are now planning to get a full-time caregiver to look after her."

"It's so dark in here," said the lawyer, looking around. "Why don't you open those curtains? All the three egress windows are quite large. Allow some light into this room, make it cheerful."

"No, no," Janet said. "Mom doesn't want any light. She always liked to sit in darkened rooms after dad's passing."

All lies, all lies! I wanted to scream that I don't like the dark. I used all my strength to squirm and twist, then opened my mouth wide and spat. I blinked and blinked and tried to fall out of the bed.

"See, this is what she does most of the time," Janet said, coming to my bed and pretending to adjust my pillow and quilt. "It's okay, mom. We won't open the curtains. We know you like it this way."

The lawyer must have sensed something was amiss. He told Derek, "Hey, we will need a doctor to certify that her cognitive abilities have been affected and that she cannot walk or speak again or act in an independent manner. We will need that before we try to obtain a power of attorney document. There could be a mountain of legal troubles for you, otherwise. Why don't you take her to the heart and stroke unit and get a current medical certificate?"

"We did that a year ago, just after she had the stroke. The doctors then said her condition would improve in a couple of months. It has been a year now - there is no change in her condition. Things are getting worse. Unfortunately, there is no hope," said Janet. "We miss her bubbly nature so much and the children adore her and want to be with her, but she can't respond..."

Lies, intolerable lies...These diabolical creatures are fruits of my womb... These monsters. Now, did I change my will three years ago? I am certain that I did. I think I did... Yes, Mary Jane knows about me. These degenerates must not get a red cent. My memory is a little distant... I did sign some papers to give the money away...to whom? Did I? There are papers. Yes, Mary Jane, yes...

Now the execution plan. On Friday, when the long weekend begins, all the grandchildren will be sent to a weekend camp early in the morning. They wouldn't want any laughter and shrieking at the time of an important ritual—a high-point in their wretched lives, wouldn't they?

My son Derek will first slather my head with several cups of olive oil and then pour buckets and buckets of cold water over me... I will shiver and scream, but no sound will pass my lips.

They will sit me in a semi-comatose state in the icy tub for a few hours and carry me back to my bed. My loving daughter Janet will then force glutinous sugar water down my throat. Three or four or more glasses of it. I am a diabetic.

I have heard them say that this will soon induce a high fever, create an electrolyte imbalance in the bloodstream and spark epileptic seizures that will shut down my kidneys, my liver and whatever is left of my brain in about two days and I will die without pain. I can't stop it.

I hear Derek and Janet come down the stairs.

"Hey Mom," he shouts. He sounds as if he is celebrating something and both of them stand by the side of my bed. Cheryl is standing near the stairs, trying to appear invisible in the shadows. She is carrying a plastic bag full of ice, and there is another bag at her feet.

I stare at my children with unbearable sadness; I choke up and my rheumy eyes are wet with tears.

Derek turns to his sister and says, "Don't fret, Janet, everything will work out fine."

He pulls the quilt off my withered frame.

My old-time friends at the Seniors' Recreation Center will talk about me on Tuesday afternoon, while enjoying their dainty cucumber sandwiches and blueberry muffins in the lunchroom.

"Oh, did you hear? Andrea died last night." Eileen, always the first to announce happenings in the community, will be a little emotional. "She has been ailing for some time, you know. She was only 78 and they say it was multiple organ failure. And her memory…It's so sad …But her kids will now be very wealthy."

Elizabeth will nod her head in agreement. 'Yeah, kidney, pancreas, liver, brain, all gone, I heard. It was all so sudden. She has been ailing for a year now. Tsk... tsk... Her children were so much attached to her, they adored her. Derek and Janet wouldn't even let us visit her, saying it'll be upsetting for her."

"Yes," Sarah will say. "Andrea didn't recover after the stroke. I met her last year. She went downhill very fast. I remember how she was always going on and on about her children and grandchildren in the early days. I wish I had such a great family to look after me."

Across the table, Mary Jane was engrossed in her phone, her thumbs moving with speed on the keypad.

"Are you here with us, Mary Jane?" asked Sarah. "Have you

nothing to say about Andrea? You were very close to her and you were the only one who saw her a couple of times after her stroke, weren't you? Did you hear anything from the family about the funeral arrangements?"

Mary Jane shook her head. "It's all about castles in the air, crumbling cookies, shattering of dreams... It's all dust."

"What are you mumbling about, Mary Jane? I was talking about the funeral."

"No, I don't have any information yet," Mary Jane said and was back on her phone.

I have that appointment at the lawyer's office in another hour, and then it's off to the police station to see Detective Ian Murphy of the Homicide Division. Tomorrow morning, I will meet with the administrator of the Mount Sugar Palliative Care Centre on Chesterfield Road and the Chair of the Board at the Heathington Long Term Care Home. They will be thrilled with the rich bequests coming their way.

Mary Jane pushed back her chair and got up. "Oh, I have to leave now. Something urgent has come up... By the way, Andrea's funeral could be many days away...There are some complications... Brace yourselves, I will tell you all about it tomorrow evening."

A Bad Day On The Trail

Jeremy screamed and ran like a bull goaded by an electric prod. One of two unleashed dogs had pounced upon him as he encountered them in the middle of the trail—they must have come down from the yard of one of the ravine homes. The taller dog with ears pinned back had chased him on one side while the shorter, meaner one with larger teeth had jumped from the other and bitten his left ankle. He had tried to fend off the dogs, and the taller dog sank its fangs into his right wrist. The pain was excruciating, and he had never experienced such terror in his life.

Run, don't think, run.

The dogs were snarling and closing in again.

The trees on either side of the Bull's Head Loop Trail on the Bruce Peninsula were ghostly this mid-March evening, waiting for the dusk that would descend with unkind speed. This was a trail on which he made a brief run in October last year, when the woods were rich with shades of gold, red and brown. It was a gratifying jog at the time and he had met several hikers and runners on the way.

But today, he had felt a sense of desolation at the start of the run. There were only bare branches of massive trees, their roots criss-crossing through the topsoil of the forest floor. Broken boughs were everywhere.

I should not have come here today. Run, don't think... run.

Crazed with fear, Jeremy hurtled through the trees, leaping and falling through prickly brush. Thorns punctured and ripped his skin through his joggers and T-shirt. Now deep in the woods, he couldn't find any trail. The dogs were about ten feet behind him. He was bleeding from his ankle and finding it difficult to run. He heard a faint whistle in the distance. The dogs stopped chasing him, perked up their ears and disappeared into the shadows, growling.

Blood oozed from his ankle and wrist, thin ribbons of ripped skin hung down his arms and legs and he found it difficult to walk. He stumbled on a charred tree stump and fell flat on his chest. He wheezed and coughed, gasping for air as he got up.

C'mon, breathe in slow, breath out slow, breath in, breath out. Breath in... Fuck!

Jeremy leaned on the trunk of an old-growth beech tree. He took off his headband and tied it tightly around his swelling wrist that had many inches of skin ripped off. In the gloom of the approaching twilight, Jeremy could see trees all around him. He removed the shoe from his left foot. The blood from the ankle had clotted on his socks. The wound looked deep, but the foot had gone numb with the running. He removed the sock and bound it round the ankle. He began limping and then hurried through the decaying leaf litter on the forest floor... Chipmunks jumped and scattered, and his heart jumped when something flashed above his head.

Oh, a flying squirrel. Where are the people...? Okay, must be careful now. Should not have taken this route. Should have gone up the ravine...There were homes there... No markings on the trees here... There could be bears in the area... Somewhere down should be another trail, a stream or a road...

"My God, my God," he panted. "I need water, I need water."

Where's my phone... I had it strapped on my arm... Gone when I hit that tree... I think... Can't go back... And my watch... Gone.

The ground had become rough and strewn with pebbles. The woods were cooler, and the light was fading fast, although a patchy blue sky was still visible through the birch trees and the pines. There was no wind, no sounds of screeching owls, no chatter of spring cicadas, no gekkering of foxes—only the sound of twigs and dried branches crackling under his feet. He felt a wave of foreboding wash over him, something ominous ahead, a flash in the mind of impending death. He could see eyes gleaming at him from every tree. Jeremy realized he was now becoming delirious.

My clients... What about these things? Unpredictable. Nothing is linear...Vertical investment broker... Get to the other side... Here I am... Swimming... My life... My wife... Jogging for years and nothing like this...There are pebbles...Where is the creek? Breathe deep... Breathe in...

Jeremy gasped as he pushed through the shrubs and hit out at the bare, hanging branches of the trees as the ground climbed and dropped every few steps. He scrambled to get over some rocks, after stepping into a shallow crevice full of rotting leaves that covered his shoes like jelly. Pain shot up from his left ankle into his hip. Fluffy, aerial roots of poison ivy brushed against his face and neck. He was now itching and scratching all over. Bile rose in his throat. He stopped. His right hand was swelling and turning blue; he twisted the headband and tightened it on his wrist. The tiny lacerations on his arms and all over his body were now beginning to burn.

He took a turn to the left and saw three white-tailed deer near a dense thicket of spruce, cedar and high bushes. They were watching him, still and silent, like the surrounding air. He moved, twigs snapped under his feet, and the spooked deer leaped together and disappeared down an incline.

There were deer resting, so there can't be a bear nearby. It must be about six or seven in the evening now. I am losing sense of direction and time... Must have been lost for over three hours. Where are the access points in these unending woods? Which way now? Go down, go down... Down... Like the deer did... Don't run diagonal...

The last, melancholic light of dusk had melted away, and he was now trapped inside a capsule of darkness. Baffling sounds were rising from the forest floor and the trees.

Jeremy thought of money—stacks of $100 bills packed tight in a duffel bag in the spare tire compartment in the trunk of his car, the $80,000 he had skimmed off customers' accounts. He had another hundred grand that he was handling for a client whose business he knew nothing about. All bundled and wrapped in waterproof, heavy-duty plastic which was taped low down on the engine fire wall.

Oh my God, that necklace, the diamond necklace I bought for Julia, is under the passenger seat. Julia, my secretary with the lovely skin, lovely legs and lovely everything. Fuck... And all that money has to reach the Cayman Islands the day after. I have to reach the car soon. Okay, I still have the car key... Good... Now get on a trail somehow... And get to a doctor.

Stumbling through the underbrush, Jeremy crashed into gnarled trees, his arms flailing like a swimmer in a pool, grimacing with the pain searing through his limbs. Icy fingers of fear crawled across his neck and chest when he heard the staccato yips of coyotes. A short howl sounded very close. His thigh and leg muscles tightened as he flung himself forward, blind now in the rush to flee from the area. Sliding down a sloping, rocky outcrop, he fell on his hands and knees onto flat, squishy ground.

Jeremy was now at what seemed to be the edge of the woods. The trees were not clustered together like the scary, stifling forest that he had just crossed. The trunks were thinner and not very tall. There were more of honeysuckle bushes with branches like tentacles of some monster creature waiting for its prey. Chopped and charred branches were scattered across the ground. A musty odor of decaying wood hit his nostrils.

Hope at last. What a relief. I am out... Breath in... Breathe out...

I have come down from the spine of this accursed land, this bloody escarpment. Fuck me, fuck me... I am not coming here again... Must find a doctor... Must take a shower... Must reach my car...

Out of the woods now, Jeremy pushed aside the bushes and saw farmland and a clearing ahead. Peering into the darkness, he spotted the silhouette of a minivan under some trees at a distance, its parking lights on. Panting, his mouth dry like sandpaper, he limped through the thin, white fog towards the vehicle.

"Help, help." He tapped on the window. The glass lowered halfway and a young man hissed, "Piss off, asshole." He heard a girl giggle inside. The window closed. He tapped once more. The window opened again. A fist shot out and caught him on the nose. Jeremy staggered back, holding his jaw with both hands. "Bastard," the youngster yelled. The girl giggled again.

What kind of people are these...? What do I do now? The McCurdy parking lot is somewhere in the middle of the loop trail. I don't think I can walk to the car... It must be miles away... And which way should I now go to get some help...?

He used his shirt to wipe away the blood tricking from his nose. A couple of dim yellow lights twinkled at least a kilometer away; and he hobbled headlong into a rural residential area. 'Little Pine Drive' he read on a road sign. There was nobody around, only scores of mature trees, their branches still comfortable in their winter hibernation. Widely separated, the houses appeared shrouded in a veil of black lace. Light shone in some windows. The fog was now thickening, and a chill filled his lungs.

Should I knock or ring the bell at one of the houses?

A vehicle rounded a bend in the distance, racing in his direction on the unpaved road, its headlights cutting a wide swathe through the darkness. Jeremy stepped onto the gravel, waving. A large black pickup truck with an extended cab stopped beside him.

"Whassup, man?" asked the driver, rolling down his window. He was a young man of maybe 20 or 22, with a baby face.

Oh well... What a relief... He is about my son's age.

"I have been bitten...Two dogs," the words tumbled out. "Can you get me to a hospital...? I need a doctor. Some water... Please?" On the verge of collapsing, Jeremy grabbed the side of the pickup. "Do you have a phone?"

The driver and two other young men got out of the vehicle. "Hey, this guy says a dog chomped him," the driver said. "Big dogs, yeah? Did them get your balls?"

They all laughed and surrounded him. A fat man, with a big belly, poked him in his stomach."Where you from, man? You have a name?"

"My name... name is Jeremy. From Caledon. Can you help me?" he rasped. The words came out with difficulty. "I was running on the Bull's Head trail and got lost. Help me please. Give me some water please... I need a doctor."

"Hey, my name's Jeremy too," the driver smirked. "Caledon is far out, man. It's behind them mountains and them rivers and them fields. Yeah, a long way, man." They all laughed. "This is outer side of the moon, man."

The driver walked around Jeremy. "No shit, this guy been scratched; he is bloody bleeding... Okay man, doncha worry. We'll get you to hospital soon. Give him a drink, fatso and take out that first aid box." He moved away and opened the passenger side door of the pickup. "Get in, man..."

"Yes, yes, thank you. Yes, thank you... I will give you some money. Cash, if you get me to the hospital."

The driver closed the door. His tone changed. "You wanna give us money?... You have the cash on you? Cheese, man, cheese?"

"A thousand bucks, two thousand…" Jeremy's voice was hoarse. "I can give you more. Just help me. Where am I now?"

"A thousand, two thousand bucks for each...? Yeah?" He looked at the others. "Hey, we got an asshole; a fatcat here ... Says he can shit out the cash... Where's the money, babbo?"

"It's in my car... Somewhere on the trail. Take me to the hospital and I will give you the money later..."

"Okay, let's round it up...You give us ten fucking grand total. No hassle? No double deal, no ducking..."

"Yes... yes," Jeremy said, his voice rising. "I am in pain... Take me to a hospital, you third-rate bums, instead of just standing and talking...Talking about money... You, bloody pieces of shit. I can buy all of you and your grandmothers."

The driver moved away and the three men huddled close, whispering to each other. The driver said, "Hey fatso, give him some water first... And then frisk him."

The fat man handed over a half-empty bottle of cola to Jeremy. Without warning, before even the bottle touched his mouth, the youngster who was on the passenger seat of the pickup leaped at Jeremy, and punched him on the side of his head. "Want my grandmother, eh?" Jeremy fell backward, his head hitting hard on the clumpy shoulder of the road. He tried to scream, but couldn't.

"C'mon, dawg." The driver pushed the puncher aside. "No beatings, okay? We need to get his car, man. Asshole looks a nasty boob... He will try to lam us. Must get his cash first," he said.

He leaned over Jeremy. "You okay, daddy? Here, drink this." He poured some of the cola into Jeremy's mouth and then turned towards the others. "C'mon, haul him up. Quick. Lezzgo..."

They lifted him and heaved him onto the back row of the extended cab. Jeremy was in a daze and he felt someone pull his wallet out of his tattered joggers while another pair of hands yanked his gold chain off his neck.

Jeremy heard a man say, "Not much cash here. Only a ten-dollar note. There's a bank card, a credit card and a car key. Hey, wow, this fucking wanker has a bloody Jaguar. Look at this key. We love you man..."

The driver prodded him. "Where is the car? How did you land here? Where did you park?"

"I don't remember... I don't know... Somewhere in the Tobermory area," spluttered Jeremy, holding the side of his head. Pain had given way to fear. "Just let me go and I will get you the money. Give me a phone or call for an ambulance. Please."

Can't let them find the car. All that money... I will be ruined.

"The weasel's lying. No way, he ran all the way from Tobermory. Nobody can. Not through the woods in the night," the young puncher scoffed. "Black bears and coyotes and foxes in there. How they not catch him? Why he not fall on rocks and break his bones? Lying asshole."

"Please please..." His cries came out in a torrent. "I got lost on the trail. Don't do this. I can give you a lot of money... Please, give me a phone and some water. Please."

"Price is now five fucking grand for each of us, yeah?" the driver asked, slowing down. "Where is the car and the money?"

"Yes, yes... Yes. Five G for each... I have the money in the car. It's somewhere on the trail. Take me to the trail," stammered Jeremy.

"Yeah? Fuck, tell us where the car is, man... We'll take you there and then the hospital. You're now our fucking bitch, man. We own you. We will get your fucking stash."

The driver drove up a ridge and then down a steep slope. He turned towards the young man who was on the passenger seat. "This guy is a jerk...Won't spill it about his bloody car...We gotta hunt for it on the trail from here to over there in Tobermory."

They drove through several gravel roads through the thin woods for about twenty minutes, the path ahead lit by four high-beam lights of the pickup.

"We'll take a short-cut to the trail," said the driver. "This ATV track should get us a long way." He turned towards an incline and sped up through the bumpy track.

"Help... Help," Jeremy shouted.

The fat man, who was on the back seat, got up, pushed Jeremy down and sat on his chest. "Nobody to hear you, asshole." He pummelled Jeremy on his throat and bloodied face. He took out a gob of gum from his mouth and shoved it into Jeremy's left ear. "Tell us... Where's the car?"

"I don't know...Take me to a hospital, please. I want to see my wife. I want to see my children," Jeremy whimpered. "Please let me go." He coughed up blood and one of his eyes was now half shut.

"Shit, what's that stink, Fatso? You farted or what, buffalo?" the driver yelled as he stopped the pick-up on the mountain track.

"Fuck, this guy has shit his pants," the fat man made a barfing sound, lifted himself off Jeremy's chest and punched him in his stomach. "Fuck, he is now peeing..."

"Hey guys, open all the windows... He stinks worse than a skunk... Did he eat a rat or what?" asked the driver.

The fat man squeezed Jeremy's groin. "Hey, this fucker is feeling horny... His cock is up." The man tightened his grip, as Jeremy squirmed."Your wife is good lay, yeah? She hot?...You thinking of the whore? Does she suck good, you fucker? " He crashed his massive fist on the side of Jeremy's head. "Bloody turd."

Jeremy's head wobbled, and he went inert, his mouth wide open.

"Oh fuck, oh shit. Something happening to this prick. He's not moving, man. I think he's dead!" yelled the fat man, slapping Jeremy on both sides of his face. "Fuck, get up, you... Get up. Open your eyes. C'mon, c'mon...!"

The pickup stopped. The driver got out, opened the rear door, and poked at Jeremy's chest. He thrust his fingers up Jeremy's nose. "What have you done, fatso? What the hell? There's no air in his nose...You bloody blipped him. Shit, we needed him to find his car. The asshole said he had a bundle of money in the car. Now, it's up the shit creek, man. Big job for us."

The three men stood leaning on the side of the pickup. "We can't drive around with this stiff," the driver said. "And, we are on an ATV trail. Our pickup will have a rough time... Can't go far."

He lifted the tonneau cover off the pickup's cargo bed and took out a bottle of beer from a cooler bag. He opened it, drank half of it and said, "Hey, anybody wants a beer?"

"No, no, later. Have to get rid of the body first," said the young man who had thrown the first punch at Jeremy. "It's already two in the morning. And fatso, you better clean out the blood and all that shit from the seat. You did that..."

"Say, should we throw him off the cliff at Indian Head Cove... like that other guy last year?" asked the fat man. He had lost his bravado and was now rubbing his hands together. "What do we do... What do we do?"

"Let's push him down a ravine...Critters can tear him out," said the young puncher. "And then go look for his car and find all that money."

"No, no. We'll take him to the Grotto and throw him into Cyprus Lake... they found a body last week at Indian Head Cove. So the cove is out. Too dangerous," said the driver. "The ravine is no good. Some freaky trekker or an asshole like this one might find it."

"Yeah, Cyprus Lake is good," said the puncher. "Muddy water most of the year, except summer. Nobody goes camping or boating until July. And the grotto is all barred up."

"Anybody need a bump before we go?" asked the driver, taking out a small plastic packet from his jacket. He put three railings of the white powder on the bonnet of the pickup and snorted one into his nose. He rocked his head and sniffled. The other two men joined in.

"Can I get one more?" asked the fat man.

"Later, fatso," the driver said. "After we flush away this piece of shit... He called us shit and wanted to screw our grandmothers."

Jeremy was limp as they pulled him out of the pickup and was thrown to the ground. There was no response to kicks on his arms and head. "Yeah, yeah, he is total dead," said the fat man.

"We know that, fat dumbo, you idiot. We'll dump him on the west side. That's a no-go place, with all them algae and bullrush," the driver said.

They dragged Jeremy through the soggy, dormant grass, pushing aside the tall reeds. The inky murkiness of the starless night merged with the dark and opaque waters. Jeremy was semi-conscious as they launched him head first into the lake. The thin layer of ice shattered into fine shards and sharp slivers, and Jeremy suffered a thousand pinpricks and slashes.

"It's fucking cold. Lezzgo and hunt for the bastard's car. Better we find it before the sun comes up," said the driver as the others piled into the pickup. "It has to be some shit place on the trail. Any ideas about parking lots of these bums?"

"We'll find out. We now have enough time," the puncher said. "This bloody fatso ruined our easy chops day."

The pick-up changed course and sped towards an unpaved road that intersected with a hiking trail a few kilometers ahead.

Rain fell, mixed with sleet. A flash of lightning raced overhead and the rumble of thunder rolled across the lake. The muddy water came alive and rippled as Jeremy rose and waddled through it, thrashing his arms around, covered in wriggly water reeds and slime. He stumbled as he made his way towards the shore. A faint, yellow light beckoned from afar, like a single planet in a misty sky.

There must be somebody there... Is it a park office or some shed?.

Half blind, with his left eye popped out of its socket, his broken jaw hanging low… his larynx fractured and his voice gone… his nose dripping blood, Jeremy tried to stand on the soft, wet earth. The rain was now heavier. Shivering, he clambered up the wooden boardwalk on his hands and knees, and dragged himself through a tangle of bushes towards a heap of stones. Dogs howled in the distance.

More dogs? Now what...?

Did he step on something slippery... slithery?

A high-pitched rattle buzzed in the clump of grass near his left ankle. A searing sensation pierced through his skin, muscles, and bones. It throbbed, and exploded in his skull.

"Oh God," Jeremy gurgled, as he collapsed; and the bitter wind seized his breath and moved on.

The Party

I am standing at the edge of the sidewalk, trying to stay steady. The road looks eerie; it seems some distance away and the water streaming into a storm drain looks beautiful. It's a nice little stream. When you look at the shimmering water, you can see the glow from the street lamps. No, it's the light of the moon, reflecting in the small waves, undulating... as it flows through the gravel-covered plains.

What are these lamps—green, blue, silver and red—flickering away at high speed? They all seem so far away. Luminous, in a hazy way.

The world is spinning, and it's difficult to keep my balance. I am so wet. Am I swimming? Watch me as I move forward, move backward, shift to the left, and shift to the right. Ah, this is fun. Let me try it again. Move forward, move backward, move forward, move backward...What were those pills I swallowed at the rave party in there?

Move forward, move backward, move forward... Thud!

I can hear screams and the sound of sirens. Pinpoint lights burn into my eyes as I feel my life force ebbing away. In a sort of sticky way. It's not that nice little stream of water I saw a long time ago. Not a stream...It's a gutter. Strange. I can't feel my limbs.

"The guy fell from that apartment balcony on the third floor; must have been on a stool or the railing getting wet in the rain," I heard someone say before the blackest of darkness wove a tight cocoon around me.

"He's going to survive," the paramedic said to his colleague as they set up an IV in the ambulance. "But I don't think he will ever walk again. His neck, spine and legs are gone. Poor sod."

It's All In The Mind, Or Is It?

Hush, little baby, don't say a word,
I will have to kill you with my sword.
Up goes the spider, up on the spout,
Up goes this blade, into your snout.

The child screamed as the six-inch blade went into her nose, slicing the delicate nostrils apart, blood spraying like a thin fountain, into the sinus and up into the brain. She shook as if she was being electrocuted and then fell silent. Dead.

*****

Now, dear reader, you must be wondering what is happening here? I must explain, I will explain. First, let me tell you that Sarah is not a baby. She is a monster-child of about four years old. You don't have to worry, however. There is no need to call the police or shrinks or asylum wardens or whoever. I have not killed Sarah, although I fantasize about it often.

Our story began some sixty years ago, in the central Ontario town of Gravenhurst, in the beautiful Muskoka Lake region. There was a wonderful little house, painted blue, just off Steamship Bay Road, with aluminum sidings and windows. Its small porch overlooked Sterling Lake, one of the pretty little lakes in the area. The lake was surrounded by ancient woods, and it teemed with fish.

A little distance away was the Larkway Pioneer cemetery which is now closed. There were enormous trees there, and I was buried near one of those huge elms, in an unmarked grave.

"She killed me," I told my wife Lisa, pointing at baby Sarah.

"Everybody in the Gravenhurst of the 1960s knew she killed me, robbed me and fled the province."

"What are you saying, George? Do you have any idea what you are saying? Sarah is our granddaughter," my wife remonstrated.

"Her name was Tamara, and she was my neighbour," I insisted. "She feigned interest in me, coming into the house alone at odd hours when her parents were off at work or leaping over the short, trimmed boundary hedge whenever she felt like it—with us ending up on the couch and kissing and cuddling."

"You are fantasizing, George."

"No, no, Lisa," I said. "I thought we had a good thing going. I even considered proposing to her, once my job as a boat machinist at the Penetanguishene docks became permanent and I could put an end to some of my quick-money deals."

I followed my wife into the kitchen. "Lisa, you must listen to me. I am not mad. One evening, one dreary winter evening, I told Tamara that I didn't like the things I was hearing about her at the marina and why some ruffians were talking about her as an easy lay.

"'They use the choicest words to describe you, Tamara, and that you cost only ten dollars,' I told her. 'I want nothing to do with you anymore. You are a whore!' She did not utter a word. Minutes later, she crept behind me, hitting me on the head several times with a claw hammer and I bled to death in front of the fireplace."

I reached up to feel the bump on the back of my head, a bump my parents said I had when I was born in Pembroke in 1963, nine months after my murder.

"It's all coming back to me, Lisa, in bits and pieces, all those little fragments of dreams from many years, now getting stronger; a kaleidoscope coalescing into solid memories."

"You are now beginning to have those nightmares during the day, George," Lisa frowned and shook her head. "Where are you getting all these fancy words? Let me call the doctor. You must see him again and ask for some medication for your anxiety. You are going on and on like some Tibetan or Bhutanese lama about a past life. Or some Hindu born-again yogi or something. What nonsense!"

Sarah was playing with a fluffy toy bear in the corridor. "Just look at her, George, look at her," Lisa said. Looking up at us, Sarah cooed, "Grampapa, Grammama." She had a bewitching smile and her eyes lit up. She waved the bear at us.

"We have such a lovely child in the family." Lisa's voice was like a spooky echo in my ears.

"I see flashes of light. I see luminous beings lurking in the shadows, trying to warn me about something. I am not becoming unhinged, Lisa. I even remember the dress Tamara was wearing fifty-nine years ago. It's all coming into sharper focus now. It was a red skirt with a black and white check blouse. It was hazy for a long time, but in recent days … in recent days …This soul is cunning. I can feel her scheming. I can see it in her eyes."

My voice faltered. I was becoming a little agitated.

"George, don't forget we are living with our son and his family," my wife grumbled. "We are broke and have no other place to go, as you know. You sold our home, destroyed our savings with your rotten investments and now this … This ranting about our only granddaughter."

"You are foolish, Lisa. You don't have any inkling of things beyond your little world." I waved her away.

Lisa raised her voice. "I am going to talk to Thomas about this. Our son has to know about his father's mindless talk and madness. He has already mentioned a couple of times that you seemed to be hazy about events that happened even two years ago. This can't go on and you better meet with the doctor."

I glared at her. "Never, ever tell Thomas about our conversations." The kitchen was hot as my temper rose. I smashed a dinner plate on the counter and stormed out.

Going into our room, I rummaged through my drawers and took out the *Gravenhurst Post* edition, dated January 26, 1963, which I filched from the Gravenhurst Public Library some months ago. Although wrapped in plastic, the paper was yellowing and looked brittle. I opened it gingerly to page 3 and showed the brief report to Lisa, who had followed me into the room. "Read Lisa, read. See what I told you."

Drug-Dealing Local Mechanic Killed

Penetanguishene: A part-time mechanic at the Pene-tanguishene docks, John M. Glover, 26, was bludgeoned to death with a claw hammer last evening. His body was found this morning, in the living room of his home on the east bank of Sterling Lake by a friend, with whom he commutes to work every day. Sheriff Moe Girard said preliminary investigation indicated that it was a woman behind the killing and that robbery could have been the motive.

Glover had no bank accounts and is believed to have hoarded a considerable sum of cash in his bedroom. Floor-boards had been removed and a part of the wall torn down. A couple of $1,000 bills were found behind the wall. All rooms were found ransacked.

The police knew Glover and suspected him of dealing in bulk quantities of marijuana and being involved with out-of-town gangs. However, sources said he was trying to turn his life around and that he was a good worker at the docks. Investigations are continuing. Glover has no surviving next of kin, Girard said.

Glover will be buried in the public corner of the munici-pal cemetery, far away from the private or reserved burial grounds, after the post-mortem and other police procedures.

"Look, that's my picture in the report. See the forehead, and just look at the nose. They are just like mine."

"Come on, George. When you were 26, it was 1989, and we got married that year. Did I marry a dead man? I don't know where you are getting these ideas from. I must call the doctor now. And... And what were you, a drug peddler?"

"Yes, I was 26 when I was killed in 1963. Yes, I was 26 when we got married in 1989. There is no connection between the two," I tried to explain. "I was conceived on January 25, 1963—the day John Glover was killed. I was reborn. Don't you see any link? Why is your mind so closed?"

Lisa doesn't understand. What I feel today is an unconscious bond with myself in a past life. It's like a cycle. Life and death, like our seasons. We come and go and come again. Since childhood, I have had this acute pain on the back of my head, whenever I felt somebody coming up behind me.

In recent days, when sitting on the porch or puttering around in the garden, I often feel the saltiness of blood gurgling in my throat, its sting in my eyes, the choking on my vomit as I see myself lying on some shabby carpet a long time ago. These feelings are real. I cannot grasp them. They flicker and vanish, leaving me with rising angst and breathlessness.

Throughout my life, people have known me as a taciturn character with a limited vocabulary, so I cannot explain how I have become so eloquent in my speech. However, I know for sure that John Glover was a loquacious man who could hold the interest of his listeners. On my occasional evening visits now to the pub in our Orangeville neighbourhood, I can hold forth a stimulating conversation on any subject and quash all arguments, uttering words which few people understand.

No wonder Lisa seems so worried. She keeps asking: "Why here, why now, why you?"

This is the same question I ask myself: "Why here, why now, why me?" It's an ontological problem for which there's no interpretation.

Gravenhurst Post, edition dated June 5, 1963:

Trail Cold In Local Mechanic's Murder

Penetanguishene: Sheriff Moe Girard yesterday informed reporters that the investigation into the murder of Sterling Lake resident John Glover, who was killed in his home on January 26 this year, had reached a dead end.

The prime suspect in the murder is his neighbor, 30-year-old Tamara McGregor, who disappeared on the day of the crime. It is believed that McGregor fled the province with a large amount of cash, taken from Glover's home.

Glover was a local mechanic with gangland connections. Her parents have no information and haven't heard from her for months. In fact, they said they were happy that she had gone away from their lives.

* 'Yes, our daughter was wild, uncontrollable,' her father, Monty McGregor, who works for the City Parks Department, said. 'She was into drugs, into men, and we don't know what else. We have nothing to do with her.'*

* Gerard said he has had no new information about her whereabouts from police forces across the country.*

All these years on, it's as if John Glover had never existed. I have checked. In Gravenhurst, the little blue house is long gone. In the sixties, a resort and an upscale residential community took over many houses and surrounding areas. Today's Gravenhurst is not the sleepy town it was in those days.

I feel within me that Tamara died four years ago, somewhere in the Maritimes, and she has reincarnated as my granddaughter. I know about it. Look at the way Sarah angles her face when she looks at me. She doesn't blink. She stares into me and through me and I have to take deep breaths to ward off panic attacks.

She is the same evil soul born in the flesh again, a spirit that has just donned a new body, like a garment. Powerful emotions can travel with the soul through many births and be part of the transmigration process. I tell you, Sarah's soul, fixated on that murderous moment of decades ago, awaits some sort of spark to attack me again.

By the age of two she had learnt to spit at me, whenever I got close to her, and to poke me in the eye when I lifted her from her crib. She is cunning, yes. She snarls at me like a vicious wolf when nobody is looking; oh, the sweet little thing, the darling little girl with the pretty brown curls, the angelic Sarah.

Some days ago, as I sat in an armchair in the living room, Sarah ran towards me and stabbed me on my hand with a table fork. I was wearing a full-sleeved, flannel shirt, so there was only minor bruising. I am certain I heard her say 'Fuck you' in a squeaky voice. She then turned around and danced away, stopping after a few steps. She pirouetted thrice on her toes, held her hands above her head, with the palms like a snake's hood, and hissed at me.

Again, on another day, I was reading a book and my wife was dawdling about in the yard when I heard a barking sound behind me. There was Sarah, crouched on her hands and knees; she then zipped around my chair at breakneck speed—round and round—and stopped suddenly in front of me. It was a terrible sight; she was doing a headstand and snarling. Yes, a four-year-old doing a head-stand! Who would believe me if I talk about these incidents?

Sarah is now prancing around in the other room, playing with her devilish rattles and God knows what is coursing through her brain. I will never touch her, never coo into her ears, never play grandfather games with her.

I know that one day she will kill me. Again.

The bell rang. It was our son Thomas and his wife Janet, return-ing from one of their many recent, extended outings. They have been wandering too much these days, leaving us to baby-sit their accursed daughter. "Hey Dad, hey Mom," Thomas called out. He sounded exuberant. "I've got the Marine Engineer's job I applied for a month ago. And surprise, surprise...We get to move away from Orangeville. We've found a wonderful new home. You'll both love it. It's large and bright, providing Sarah with ample room to run around as she grows older. And there is a big tool shed for you, Dad. We signed off on all the documents today."

"Oh," I said. "Oh."

My wife clucked around in the kitchen, putting on the kettle and taking the cups out from a cupboard along with some ginger snaps for tea, as Janet went to check on Sarah.

"This home has a lovely porch, and is just off Steamship Bay Road." Thomas was exultant as he circled around the room, keen to hear some words of approval. "The only problem is that it's near the south end of the town cemetery with its huge elm trees. But it's also right on the shore of the beautiful Sterling Lake. It's pretty, with stunning views of the awesome countryside in Gravenhurst, you know, in the Muskoka region."

Spare The Rod

The sound of the doorbell was jarring, like a screech of protest. Jazmin was in the kitchen, chopping up some carrots for a yogurt-based salad. She had reached home only a half hour ago from her work at the cash counter of a big box store. It was almost six o'clock.

Who could be calling at this time? If it's some salesperson, I will have some choice words for them. I am so drained.

"Yes?" Jazmin asked the two well-dressed people at the door.

They look like Celestial Witnesses... Always wandering around the community, hunting for souls to harvest for their congregation.

However, the couple did not seem friendly and showed none of the ingratiating mannerisms that Celestials display at the doors they knock.

"Yes, what can I do for you?" Jazmin asked.

It was the woman who answered. "Is this the Patelar residence? If you are Jazmin Patelar, we would like to come in and speak with you and Mr. Patelar. It's a rather urgent and delicate issue."

"What's this about?" Jazmin was getting impatient.

"Oh, I am sorry we didn't introduce ourselves. My name is Doreen Bennett. I am from the Children's Help Society here in Caledon and this is Jim O'Reilly. Mr. O'Reilly is a legal counsellor at the Barton District School Board."

"What's wrong? Can you tell me what's going on?" Jazmin was a little flustered now. She had one son, aged ten, and a daughter aged eight, and there were no problems at home. She and her husband had stable jobs. They had a good house with a nice yard and they loved their children, although they often threw silly little tantrums. The neighbours were great and there were never any major quarrels and her son played on the swings and slides in the parkette down the road. He was a loner, though. Her thoughts were now on a high-speed train.

"Can we come in?" Doreen's voice was intrusive.

"Yes, yes, come on in. Sit down. Oh, you can sit here, Mr. O'Reilly. Yes, on that sofa. My husband is in the yard, I will go get him. He loves to plant things every summer." Jazmin wrung her hands. "He has a green thumb and he plants squash and cucumber and eggplant and chillies and tomato every year. He is now doing what he calls aeration of the soil and what not. We get quite a lot of produce, which we distribute to our neighbours. The children have a lot of fun plucking them. I remember how last year..."

The visitors were silent, staring at her.

"Oh, I will get my husband. Would you like some coffee or tea?"

"Mrs. Patelar, we are fine, thank you. We stopped at a cafe before coming here. We will have to speak with both of you now and later have a chat with your son. His name is Varun, yes?"

Doreen removed her glasses, blew on it and wiped the lenses with an end of her scarf. She opened a binder and laid three pages on the coffee table.

Jazmin's heart skipped a beat. She was jittery.

What has Varun done now? Oh my God, did he stab some child with his compass today? Or did he hit somebody with his cricket bat? Did he take that wretched pocketknife to school? The boy seems to be going off track.

"I have told him many times not to take his cricket bat to school. Did he do something with the bat?" Jazmin waved her hands. "I will get my husband."

"Do that, Mrs. Patelar," Doreen said. "We need to meet with your son, too. Could you please call him and tell him to wait in another room while we speak with you and your husband?"

Jazmin rushed into the yard. "Kiran, there are some people from the Children's Help Society here to speak with us."

"Busybodies. They want to poke their noses into family affairs." Kiran muttered. "We are paying so much tax already, paying their salaries—and they want to go around harassing people." He washed his hands at the yard tap, wiped them with a paper towel, and walked into the living room.

"Hello, Mr. Patelar. I am Doreen and this is Jim from the Children's Help Society."

"Oh hi...What's this all about?" Kiran asked, sitting across them on a chair that he pulled out from under a work desk.

"Our office had sent you a message this afternoon about our visit. Didn't you get it?" Jim asked.

"Yes, yes, but I saw the message only about an hour ago, so couldn't respond. So, what's this about?"

"We have received a preliminary report that could be a problem for you. I mean, do you beat your son or threaten him in some way, Mr. Patelar?" Doreen was direct as she glared at him, her forehead wrinkling into a panel of parallel lines. "And where's he now?"

"My son and daughter have both gone for a movie with their cousins and uncle in Hamilton. And what are you saying? Beating? Me...my son. Jazmin, what are these people saying?"

"The Children's Help Society has received a complaint that there could possibly be some child abuse going on in this house." Doreen's tone was now conciliatory. "There is nothing to worry about. This is just a formality. We have to inquire and submit a report on every such complaint."

"This can't be. This is not true. There cannot be such a complaint from anyone," Jazmin said. She looked as if she was going to cry.

Kiran was fuming with rage. He stood up. "What nonsense is this? What the hell are you talking about?"

"Calm down, Mr. Patelar, calm down. This is an issue which could have legal repercussions," Jim, who was silent until now, said.

Doreen turned a page over in the binder on her lap and looked up at Kiran. "You could be a perpetrator, with your son as the victim. The note we received from Varun's school mentions that you could be beating up your son, maybe often, and that he is terrified of you. We want to know if this is true." There was a touch of finality in her voice.

"You must be mistaken. No such thing happens in this house. My wife and I have never laid a finger on our children. You can ask them too. We don't even raise our voices, whatever mischief they get into everyday. In India, where we come from, parents spank their children. That is how they inculcate good behaviour. They do it out of love. Teachers also use the cane to enforce classroom rules."

Kiran began pacing the room. "My father used to beat me with a belt if I disobeyed him or got low marks in a class test. In school, my math teacher used a ruler to rap students on their knuckles. Ah, but that really hurt. But, you see, we all excelled in mathematics and algebra and geometry. A little discipline is a good thing. I think that helped me to become a computer engineer and succeed in my job. I am a gold medallist from the University of Delhi."

"Will you sit down, Mr Patelar?"

"Okay, I will sit down. But do you know why there is so much indiscipline in Canadian schools? Pupils abusing teachers, showing no respect for authority or even their parents, and girls getting pregnant at the age of thirteen and fourteen—it's all because of the belief that children should be left alone to do as they please, without any guidance. And many of them become criminals, take drugs..."

Kiran paused, realizing that what he was saying was not what the visitors wanted to hear. Mr. Oreilly was glowering at him, open-mouthed, while Ms. Bennett looked sullen, her face in a frown of extreme displeasure.

Kiran changed tack. "But our family is integrated here. We don't have any cultural baggage with us. We are good Canadians. We are law-abiding and believe in dealing with our children by showering them with love and understanding. We don't threaten, we don't shout...What the heck, we don't even ground them if they don't listen to us—like white Canadian parents do."

"Well, maybe it's a misunderstanding. Three days ago, one of Varun's teachers said she was writing a note in his communication book—that he had skipped doing some homework," Doreen spoke with deliberation. "She has written that Varun started crying aloud and kept saying, 'My dad will beat me... He will thrash me with a belt or cane if you write this note.' The teacher wrote up an incident report and informed her superiors. This is the second time this has happened. The school officials did what they are required to do by law and notified us. So, you calm down, Mr. Patelar."

"I am calm, okay? I am calm." Kiran laughed and stood up. "My son is a smart boy. This is all a misunderstanding. He has lied to the teacher. I don't know why. He likes to act up. We always tell him he will be an actor in Bollywood when he grows up. We will speak with him about this when he returns from Hamilton on Sunday. This is the weekend, after all." He laughed aloud again.

"We will take leave now," said Doreen. "Can you please sit down, Mr. Patelar? Sign this document here—just a record that we visited you today. We are really sorry about this. We are just doing our job, you know. If there are any more complaints, of course, we will escalate the issue. You realize that, don't you? Your son should be told not to tell lies, if he is lying... You would have to take him to a psychologist if he keeps repeating such lies. We will be speaking with your son in school next week, since he is not here today."

"Not to worry, not to worry. We will speak with him, and his teachers as well," Jazmin said as she escorted them out and shut the door behind them.

Kiran was livid, his face flushed red. Reaching for the slender cane with a silver handle from atop the dining room hutch, he said, "Jazmin, let Varun out of the basement cupboard. Let little Vineeta also come out of our bedroom washroom and remove the tape from her mouth; at least that kept her quiet when those idiots were inside our home."

"You knew those ugly, white vultures were coming around, didn't you? You didn't tell me anything."

"I had a text message this afternoon saying that they wanted to discuss a complaint made by some stupid teacher about Varun. I came in an hour earlier to lock them up," Kiran said. "What do these people think? Meddling in family affairs... the idiots."

Jazmin nodded. "Oh, I thought it was one of those days when the kids screamed and quarreled and that you had punished them in the usual way. Both are turning out to be quite a handful. Some of these woke teachers in our schools are a bad influence on children."

Kiran ran his fingers up and down the cane. "We will make sure that Varun never utters a word about our home or family to anybody in school or elsewhere again. Woke, or no woke... He will grow up to be a smart young man, well educated and with a disciplined head on his shoulders. The same with Vineeta too. Let's go..."

"Be careful, Kiran, don't break skin," Jazmin said, as she kept pace with him, while going down the stairs.

Little Old Ladies

"I say that we castrate him," said Nellie. She is the most passionate of our lot. Sandra and Eileen, however, voted for penectomy, you know, the complete removal of the male organ.

I agreed with them. "Such parasites should never have sex again. Let the yearning churn in his head, round and round forever."

My friends and I were talking about a thug we abducted two days ago; and we are now at Sandra's cottage on Matagamasi Lake, in the Kukagami watershed in Northern Ontario, off the Trans-Canada Hwy/ON-17. It's not on the weekend holiday circuit and there are few people living in this wilderness corridor. Some anglers come to the lakeside during the summer months to catch trout, bass and perch. The lake is about an hour's drive north from Sudbury.

The brute stirred. Nellie administered an injection just below his left ear. "There Liz, this second dose should knock him out for at least eight hours," she told me, pulling hard on the ear. Nellie practiced for 40 years as surgeon's aide in the operation theatres of two well-known hospitals; I cannot tell you which ones.

Now, this may sound like a plot scripted for scores of B-grade revenge movies or C-grade pulp novels, but I have a unique imagination and like telling stories. Beware, some of them could be very tall tales!

So, continuing on with the story...We first saw this scoundrel at a cafe in Milton. He was an easy mark and we had gone over the abduction logistics over two weeks ago. I had ordered coffee when he sauntered in, his trousers belted midway on his thighs, his underwear showing. Ugh! He ordered a doughnut and sat on a chair behind me. I had already noticed his eyes lighting up as he looked me over and decided that I was a 'meek prey.'

I opened a thick brown envelope—so he could get a glimpse of the wads of hundred-dollar bills inside, as I spoke into my phone. "Yes, darling. I have the money with me. Yes, all four thousand dollars of it...What? Yes, I have it in my bag… Yes, I will take the Halton Hills Lake trail and wait at the Rattlesnake Lookout Point... Okay, meet you at 3:30 pm, sharp. You know I can't stand for long. My knees will give out with my blasted arthritis. Come soon."

The gorilla was all ears. His eyes gleamed again as he looked at me. I smiled at him. A sight to behold, as I had inserted a silicon prosthetic to hide my teeth and was gumming it. That makes me look more like a vulnerable old lady, the kind that his ilk likes to abuse by muggings, burglaries, beatings and sometimes old-fashioned rapes. We keep reading reports in the newspapers and on television about such ghastly things taking place, targeting seniors.

Sometimes, the news becomes too close for comfort. This happened to our friend Janet a couple of years ago. One night, someone attacked her in her home, viciously beating her about the head and raping her. She lost one eye and her jaw had to be wired to hold the bones in place. Poor Janet. She was 79 years old and died soon after. But Janet's friends have long memories. And they don't forgive.

"Got him," I texted on my phone and looked across the room. At the far end, Nellie and Sandra were sipping coffee. I picked up my bag and umbrella and walked out. The time was 1:30 pm. Today, I am the bait, and the hunter will learn that the bait has a vicious bite.

Let me clarify that this ruffian whom we strapped on the gurney had nothing to do with Janet. We already dealt with that villain two years ago. That is a story, a figment of my fertile mind, which I will tell you some other time. One might say that we should serve justice in a legal and humane manner. However, my friends and I are emotional beings and we think revenge is the better option. 'Preventive revenge' also should be a choice. It helps to restore some balance in this mad world.

This latest brute is that same kind of psychopath, out on bail after being arrested for several violent break-ins and assaults on seniors living alone.

Now, let us get back to the hunt and let my imagination go berserk. I left the cafe, hopped into my car and in twenty minutes reached the Halton Hills Lake trail... I watched him in the rearview mirror, following me in a shiny blue, low-slung sports car.

This isn't fair...Where do these bums get the money to live the high life? This must be a stolen car. Parasites!

I parked at the base of the escarpment and took the trail, heading uphill, pretending to stop every ten steps or so, using my straight umbrella as a cane and wheezing aloud for effect. Why should I let him know that at seventy-one, I am fitter than him and that only last month I ran the Mississauga half-marathon?

Reaching the top of the hill, I plodded to the lookout with its lush canopy of trees. The trail was lonely; it was a weekday. Joggers and strollers would start their routines only towards the evening, and the lookout point was concealed from the main trail.

"Okay, Mums, show me what you got." The bastard was panting behind me, the exertion almost doing him in.

"Hey mister, I am not your mum," I mumbled, like a toothless old woman. "What do you want?... And didn't I see you out there in the cafe?"

"Gimme that bag." His hand reached into his hip pocket and came out with a flick knife. The blade must have been about six inches long and he waved it about. "Or I will cut your throat."

"Okay, okay," I cried. "Please don't hurt me." I pouted, whimpered, and turned on my tear tap. Sandra always tells me I am a good actress.

"You want the bag? Take it," I said, tossing it high over his head.

His eyes shifted and his hands reached skyward. My umbrella handle came cleanly out of its sheath—its twenty-four inches of double-edged, cold steel flashing as it punctured and twisted inside his right lung.

Blood gurgled in the idiot's throat as he crumpled to the ground, trousers falling around his shoes. "Touche," I said, gently sheathing the Iberian Falcata blade forged many years ago by my late husband in a Texas foundry. As a rapier, it's a great thrusting blade. "Targeted penetration," I told him. "Not like your silly, little cock." He was already losing consciousness.

Two ATVs came to a halt beside me. We worked with speed. Nellie opened her medical bag, plugged his puncture with super glue and injected him with an anaesthetic. "We'll stitch him up later."

"Good job, Liz," Eileen said as we rolled him in a tarp and cleaned up the ground, pouring a large bottle of cola over the few drops of blood. Nellie's brother Conrad, who has provided us with muscle power during our many outings, carted him away on one of the ATVs down the trail to his Milton farm. Eileen and Nellie followed him on the other ATV. I trudged back to my car, removed my silver-haired wig, pulled out the prosthetic gums and headed to the farmhouse, where we burnt them in a fire pit.

After a light lunch of sandwiches and review of our plans, we started on the next portion of the saga. Pouring a tumbler full of rye whiskey into the lout's mouth and on his shirt, we strapped him into the backseat of an SUV. Just a precaution, you see. If we are stopped on the way, we could always tell a curious cop that our friend was drunk and sleeping it off. We look at all possibilities and also prepare alternate plans. It took us approximately six hours of driving to reach the cottage on Matagamasi Lake.

I hope the narrative is piquing your interest. Like I said, I have a feverish imagination that sometimes borders on hallucination.

Anyway, this is the story of the reprehensible creature. He duly underwent a penectomy, and Nellie cauterized the wound. "A flattened goon," she laughed. "I have left an opening between his anus and scrotum for him to pee. Neat work, eh?"

I used a large metal eyedropper to pour a teaspoon of sulfuric acid, taken from a car battery, into his right eye. It burned through his cornea, the iris, the sclera and whatever, and there was only a wisp of black, acrid smoke which dissipated in an instant, making him a one-eyed hood for life. No wonder this acid is called the oil of vitriol.

Sandra wanted to insert an ice-pick into both his ears to break his eardrums, but we all rejected the idea.

"No, Sandra, he must be able to listen to people enjoying life, especially when his hoodlum friends talk about sex," Eileen said.

The freak is in deep sleep now; with an eye gone, his thingummy gone, major memory loss because of the powerful sedatives injected into the back of his neck... Right in the medulla oblongata.

Conrad demanded his share of the fun. He begged us for permission to pulverize the maggot's thumbs, but we all put our foot down. "No! That's enough! That would be torture!"

We left it at that. We are not inhuman; and we ensured that he didn't feel any pain. All the equipment we used were also sterilized. Poor rascal shouldn't get any post-surgery infections.

So there! You must have read the report in a northern community newspaper about a man found wandering late one night, about three months ago in Capreol. He was near the old rail tracks on the left bank of the Vermillion River in the small town, which is way north of Sudbury. Apparently, all he could mumble were some words about a silver-haired old woman with no teeth.

I am a red-head, proud of my thick curls and my friends are not called Nellie, Eileen, Sandra or Conrad, and my name is not Liz. I must also tell you that we have no connection with any cottage on Matagamasi Lake; and I did not go to any cafe in Milton. I must say nothing more because I might incriminate my friends and myself. After all, it's just a story.

Anyway, here we are at a coffee shop at the Aspen Hill Street and McCree Road intersection this afternoon—four gentle old ladies, sipping coffee, enjoying cheese puffs and biscuits and telling raunchy stories and risqué jokes about old boyfriends.

I also have my umbrella on the floor, within easy reach. Oh, and I can see a big, brawny lout standing outside and looking at us through the window.

The Head Game

"Can you help me unscrew my head?" the passenger beside me on the Bluehorse bus said, elbowing me with some force.

We had gotten onto the bus at the Union Station bus terminal in Toronto and were off to New York. It was only about half full. It could have been the heavy snowfall warning that had deterred travellers. I was listening to a song on my iPod and the man had been scribbling in a small black book for the past 40 minutes or so.

We had just made the turn off at the Hamilton-Niagara fork on Highway 403 when he elbowed me. I tried to move closer to the window when he poked me again; this time he had an 8-inch screwdriver in his left hand. "Yes, you will help me…" It was more of an assertion than a request.

"What?" I said. "What do you want?" I was feeling scared now and my heart stepped up its tempo.

The passenger was calm, as if he was just sitting on a park bench on a sunny spring afternoon, watching children whizzing past on roller blades or young mothers with strollers or couples walking hand in hand.

Outside, the snow was whipping up a ruckus, falling thick and fast. The traffic was slowing down to a crawl. Should I shout out to the conductor and move to another seat?

"Don't panic," my neighbour whispered. "And don't get up or change your seat. I might get angry and my head will explode, you know. I could bust your gut and pull out your intestines."

I dared not look into his eyes. "Look sir, I don't understand what you are saying. I am a poor clerk at a small bookstore in the city, with no special skills. I have only a mother at home and I am not rich. Please let me move... I'll go to another seat. Please."

"Hey, hey," his voice was soothing. The other passengers might have thought we were having a pleasant conversation. He was almost a foot taller than me and with muscles like a professional wrestler. I slouched deeper into my seat.

"Hey, just listen. I need your help to unscrew my head. That is all I am asking you to do. That is why I have this screwdriver. There are copper screws that go deep into my cranium, through each of my ears."

I tried to appear calm, so as not to antagonize him.

"Do you understand?" His voice was now a whisper. "Let me make it simpler. Three years ago, I realized that this head on my shoulders is not my head."

He touched his forehead. "This head that I have been carrying around for 34 years is not mine. Somebody made a terrible mistake. They transposed heads in the hospital where I was born. And I have been searching for my property... My head, for the past three years."

He inserted the little finger of his right hand into his left ear and wiggled it, enjoying the sensation. His head was turned towards me and it seemed he was snarling at me.

"I have travelled across the country, visiting small fishing ports along the Maritime coasts and the hidden inlets of British Columbia," he said. "I have gone to lakefront resorts throughout Ontario, to the ski slopes and hot springs in the Rockies, to the beaches, and to mountain parks. I have also travelled on buses, trains and cruise ships in search of my head. Last year, I even roamed around the city of Juneau in Alaska, following a hunch."

My stomach knotted with fear as I stared at the monster screwdriver he had in his hand, pointing at me. A chill inched up my spine, like a snake uncoiling itself.

"Are you listening?" he asked, elbowing me again.

I winced.

"Sorry," he said. "I don't want to hurt you. I know you will help me. I just know it... You look like a very helpful person. You have such a gentle and foolish face. I won't bite you."

He turned towards me, showing me a mouthful of teeth. "A month ago," he continued, "I saw a man on the Sherbourne subway platform on the Bloor–Danforth line. Right in Toronto."

He paused and took a deep breath. "I was stunned. He had my head on his shoulders. Can you imagine my delight? Can you? I was ecstatic. The jawline, the curve of the nose, the shape of the ears— yes, it was my head. My three-year search had ended. I followed him onto the road, past the Ethereal Temple of God, turned into Silkweed Lane, and saw him enter one of the apartment buildings. Do you know the place? It's in the Jamiestown neighbourhood. A pleasant area. I knew then what I had to do."

He moved back and forth for a few moments and then leaned back. "A week later, I moved into an apartment on the same floor, using a fictitious name and forged documents. His name was Andrew. Yes, Andrew Becker. He had a nice family, a wife and two children, the eldest about five years or so. Yes, a compact and happy little Ontario family."

"And then... then?" I stuttered.

His reply was brusque. "I hacked the head off. Last evening, his family was away and I invited him into my apartment for a beer. I then took possession of my head. Andrew's body is in my freezer. I won't be going there anymore, anyway. Let it rot in there."

We were approaching the Canada Border Services Agency post on Rainbow Bridge and the bus was slowing down.

"That head, my head, is wrapped in plastic and it's in the blue gym bag under my seat... It's a little bloody, as it should be...," he said. I shuddered and whimpered.

"We will get down now and walk like a loving couple to the washrooms. There you will help me attach my real head to my neck. I have new copper screws and a drill. However, a drill would be noisy... I think this screwdriver would be sufficient. We'll leave this head behind the cistern or shove it inside. Okay, partner? We'll then have pleasant conversations about any subject you want—all the way to New York. By the way, my name is Sandro."

He looked around the bus and put the screwdriver away. He began nodding and whistling a popular dance tune.

The driver manoeuvred the bus to a halt in a parking bay for security and passport clearance. Some passengers were getting off to stretch their legs or go into the duty-free shop. Sandro tugged at my arm, picked up the gym bag, and herded me to the exit.

What followed must have been high-octane drama, the kind that you see only in fast-paced action movies. I don't remember much about the sequence of events. I dragged and pushed Sandro down the steps of the bus. As he fell forward, I leaped over him, ran, stumbled, fell, got up again and ran screaming towards one of the security booths, waving my hands.

"Murder, murder," I screamed. "That man is a killer. Help, help."

Several Canadian border officers rushed out, their pistols drawn, ordering me to drop to my knees and throw my hands above my head. I screamed again, "He's a killer, he's a killer."

Somebody pushed me to the ground—my jaw, chest and elbows crashing on the concrete of the parking bay. I felt a powerful jolt of electricity pass through me and I felt a knee pressed against my back, before I blacked out for a few minutes.

They handcuffed and dragged me away to one of the cabins. Scores of people—passengers from the bus and others from cars waiting for clearance to cross the border—had gathered around in a large circle and were applauding the officers. I could hear some of them shouting, 'He must be a terrorist,' 'Throw the bastard in jail,' and 'He looks like a nerd, must be a freak.'

The border officers didn't believe my story. How could they? Sandro said that his name was Brad Northmore, and he was a designer with a theatre company in New York. His blue gym bag had some costumes and masks. A rubber screwdriver which he had was a prop and couldn't hurt a fly; and he swore that he had not spoken to me at all and was busy on the bus with his notebook and pencil, sketching various diorama settings for a new stage production.

Toronto police detectives, who were contacted for the investigation, said that they accounted for all residents in the solitary apartment building on Silkweed Lane. They had received no reports of any missing person named Andrew Becker and no headless body had been found in any freezer in any of the rental units.

Three border services agents were near the door of the interrogation room, one of them obviously their superior officer. I heard one of the agents say, "The passenger whom this guy identified as Sandro said he had not spoken a word during the entire trip from Toronto. In fact, he said this character was a surly one and didn't even return his greetings soon after they got on the bus. The on-board camera also doesn't show them talking to each other. The other passengers have corroborated the Northmore story. We have checked everybody's details and documents."

The second agent, the one who tackled me from behind, said, "This guy's ID shows his name as John Higgins. Toronto police said he lives alone in a one-room apartment in Scarborough's Malvern area. He said he had a mother, but the police said his mother passed away many years ago."

Another agent said, "He has blown negative. There's no trace of alcohol or any sign of drug intoxication. The medical assistant has drawn blood for further testing. His bruised elbows and chest have been cleaned and dressed."

"Did you check the duffel bag and bags of other passengers?" the officer asked.

"Northmore's gym bag had a couple of sketchbooks and some flexible, rubber stage props. We checked him out, he is legit. He works in the theatre, most of the time in New York, but visits Toronto often. TPS said they would keep an eye on him, however. Nothing unusual was found in any other bags on the bus."

"Our detainee seems docile enough. Finish all the paperwork and get the passengers to sign individual statements. We will hand this guy over to the police. They will know what to do," the officer said. "We can let the bus and all of them go on their way. Keep me posted about this case," he said, coming into the room.

"How are you, Mr. Higgins? How are you feeling?" he asked me.

"I want to go," I yelled. "I have to be at a book show in New

York. You are holding the wrong man. Arrest that Sandro."

The border agents were looking at each other and smirking.

"Sorry, we cannot let you go on the bus," the officer said. "You assaulted a passenger. You're lucky he is not pressing charges. There are procedures to follow after your disturbing behaviour."

"My disturbing behaviour? My behaviour? He is the culprit. He is a killer. You cannot hold me. I have rights, you see. There will be problems for you if you don't let me go. I will sue you. You don't know who I am and what clout I have in high places."

The officer patted me on my back. "Take it easy, Mr. Higgins," he said, and they all left the room.

I am now at the Niagara Police detention centre, in a room with soft, padded walls and no windows. They took away my glasses, my belt, and even my shoelaces.

What do they think?...That I will flagellate myself with the shoelaces or start eating my belt or drill my nostrils with my broken eyeglass frame? Maybe I will... But it's my choice, isn't it? Idiotic cops.

Officers have photographed me from all angles, fingerprinted me, and charged me with creating mischief under $5,000 as per Criminal Code Section 430 (4). An inspector said they would take me to a police division in Toronto 'for further investigation and processing', within two days—according to my case note. A psychiatric evaluation has also been recommended. I don't know why.

Anxiety is eating away at me, and I can feel the bile rising. I feel like retching, and I am restless and afraid. I cannot get rid of the image of Sandro; I am sure that is his real name...When he got up to leave the interrogation room at the border services office, he looked at me and I could read his lips. He said, 'I will get you,' and made a slashing gesture across his throat with his forefinger.

I am also having a problem with an intermittent buzzing in my ears. It began a few days before I boarded the bus to New York. Now, I need to find somebody soon to pull out these copper screws digging into my cranium.

Stranger On The Lawn

My son Mike, who is 16 years old, is a spoilsport. He has this obnoxious habit of announcing how a mystery film ends or revealing the climax of a suspense novel. It irritates everyone in the family, especially his two younger brothers, and we have scolded him about this over the years. His explanation: 'It just happens! I have to blurt it out. Sorry!'

His mother, like all mothers, always sides with him. She just laughs it off. She is a science teacher in a secondary school and confident about dealing with children, although I don't agree with her easygoing ideas about discipline. However, we are a happy, compact family. I am a small business owner, creating innovative advertisement films with novel story lines and jingles for a select band of top clients. My friends always tell me that I am whimsical and should write full-length screenplays.

Our home is a magnet for Mike's friends, because he has a loaded up game room in the basement. It's complete with a huge television set, various consoles and gadgets, and an endless supply of finger foods and soft drinks, to keep everyone happy.

One fall evening, Mike had some of these friends in our living room. While coming down the stairs, I overheard him say, "Keep this to yourself. Your parents must never know about this, okay?"

He paused for dramatic effect. "My dad bought this stained glass panel at the Brampton Flea Market, you know, the one on Airport Road and Steeles Avenue. A real bargain; he paid only 200 dollars for it. Look at the wicked lines on the hat and the pipe and just look at the big nose and the man's Adam's apple! Doesn't it look as if it's bobbing?"

He was talking about a large and beautiful sheet of frosted glass on the front door of our home. It's a classic work of black-and-white, glazed enamel, with a bizarre story behind it.

I was a little annoyed. "Oh, you broke the secret, didn't you?"

"Sorry dad, I thought it's such an old story that you have told so many times. C'mon, don't be upset... I thought I might as well come out with the truth."

"You are incorrigible," I said, tousling his hair.

The other kids seemed amused.

"Did you really buy it from the flea market?" one of them asked. "My mom told me a different story about the door."

I raised my eyebrows, spread out my hands, snickered and walked away.

My son was a little contrite or he was pretending to be when he shouted out, "Sorry, dad, sorry!"

So let me tell you the story that has been told and retold at many of our delightful home parties.

It was a sunny afternoon on a spring day four years ago. I remember it was just before the Victoria Day long weekend began—Friday, May 10, 2020, at around 3:30 pm.

I had taken the day off from work and was on the front lawn of our large estate home in one of the new sub-divisions in Castlemore, on the north-east side of Brampton. Behind the house is a ravine with dense woods, part of the Humber River watershed. I have a remarkable green thumb and so the family kept aloof while I pottered away. In our previous home in Markham, the City twice named our front lawn as the best-kept in the neighbourhood.

That day, I was digging holes to plant some of those fancy hostas or plantain lilies, as they are called. These have attractive foliage and I knew they would look good around my young red maple tree. There was also a white hibiscus sapling, which I hoped would become a focal point in an arrangement a little distance away. I had just dug the second hole, when a dark shadow eclipsed the sun. I looked up to see a man looming over me. I hadn't seen or heard him approach and I felt an irrational fear in my gut. As a man who likes routine and is action-oriented, I don't like surprises.

The man had a black overcoat and a black fedora-like hat and must have been over six-and-a-half feet tall. He was rather lean, although the shadow suggested a man of wider girth. He had a pipe in his mouth. I tightened the grip on the handle of my shovel.

Why on earth is he wearing an overcoat when it's such a warm day? How did he get inside our gated estate community?

I tried to get up, but couldn't because he had placed his right hand on my left shoulder. It felt as though the hand weighed 30 or 40 lbs, forcing me to squat on the ground.

"Don't be afraid," he said. His voice sounded like a breeze rustling the reeds by a river bank and coming from somewhere far away. "I just want to speak with you. It's something very important to me and my family." There was a hint of menace in his voice. I couldn't see his full face, because the sun was behind him and his hat was low on his forehead. He stretched out his arm.

What the hell?

His arm seemed almost ten feet long as he pointed to our house and said, "This is my home."

I pushed his hand away and got up. He seemed to get taller, his shadow still looming over me. "This is my home and has been with my family for over 200 years," he whispered.

This guy is mad. I designed this home and got it custom-built five years ago by a reputed contractor and have all the property deeds and documents. Nonsense.

"I don't like the tone of your thoughts, sir," his voice was now huskier, like wild reeds swaying in the wind. The warmth of the afternoon vanished. "You think I am mad and that if you designed and got it custom-built five years ago by a reputed contractor and have all the property deeds and documents, it's all fine? Nonsense."

I realized with a thump in my heart that he was converting my thoughts into easy-flowing speech.

Who is this scoundrel? What new racket is this? Is this some kind of hypnotism or telepathy?

He said it aloud, "Scoundrel? This is no racket! Hypnotism or telepathy?" There was scorn in his voice.

Holy shit. This is weird.

He murmured, "What holy shit? What is weird? I can be an ugly person if you want me to be one." He shook what looked like a foot-long finger near my nose.

"You cannot plant this sort of garbage on my land." He stomped on the hosta I had just planted, mashing it into the soil. "Plant corn now and spinach in the off-season. Why have you erected this monstrosity over the foundation of my home? Where are the lovely chimneys and the small tower with its little lattice windows that were over the attic? Where is the red-tiled roof and where is the ivy that covered the walls of my beautiful home?"

His voice was fainter, as though the breeze was dying in the reeds. "I climbed the tower every evening to see the sunlight spread a golden blanket over the farmstead. There was a small orchard near the barn and a livestock pen. Gone...Where?"

Leaning closer to me, he whispered, "This is where my family lived for three generations and I will take all the steps needed to repossess my home."

He waved his arms in full circles. "I will get all the meadows and pasture too. It's our farmland and our woods. All of this. You and your kind have usurped them. "

A smell, akin to the one that I have breathed in sometimes when strolling along the banks of the Humber river, blasted my nostrils.

A damp and earthy smell, like the one you get with the first shower after a hot spell.

His mouth was near my nose. He tapped his pipe on my left shoulder. "I can be a bad man. Yes, a dangerous man."

I was now having an anxiety attack and my heart raced. My breath came out in short bursts. Although trembling as I got up, I hefted the shovel—ready to defend my family and our home. I swung it at his head. It didn't connect.

The man in the overcoat and hat was moving towards my house. He looked like a runaway horse, leaping across the lawn, and racing along the long, circular driveway.

"Hey!" I yelled. "Stop!"

I gave chase, but was far behind when he pushed the door open and disappeared into the house.

All my senses were on fire as I tiptoed with caution, fearing he could be hiding behind the door or in the powder room, ready to pounce on me. My muscles tightened, ready for action.

Holding the shovel aloft, I shouted, "Hey, get out of my house. Come on out, you. Come on out."

It was a relief that my family wasn't at home. My wife and children had left early in the morning to be with her parents in Oshawa for the weekend. I inched into the living room. Where did he go? I looked behind the sofas and then went into the kitchen, where I picked up a butcher's knife as well. One never knows how these episodes end. It's better to be safe. I shuffled through the dining room and into the family room. There was no sign of the man.

I took the stairs, a stealthy step at a time. He has to be upstairs in one of the five bedrooms.

My God, should I call 911? Or am I imagining things? Was there really a man? Let me find out, anyway.

I went through all the bedrooms, washrooms, looking under the beds, in the closets and behind the curtains. He couldn't enter the attic from the main bedroom; it was padlocked from below. I crept into the basement. There was no sign of the charlatan.

Maybe he shrank himself to hide. It's a strange world we live in. Since all the windows were locked, he couldn't have jumped outside. Where did he go?

So, I even looked into many shoeboxes and dresser drawers. Nothing! I went up to the bedrooms again.

I must tell you about the enigmatic odour of pipe tobacco that I encountered when chasing the man into my house. Friends who smoke have told me that pipe tobacco is aromatic and smells of vanilla and spices. This smell, however, triggered images of old English pubs, with polished wooden walls and floors and people cheerily drinking ale or cider, images which I have seen in period movies. It was very strong on the top floor and on the stairs but it quickly dissipated.

There was a slight sound, a pitter-patter of feet, as if a child or a small dog was running across a hardwood floor. What followed was a loud bang and the crash of splintering wood. I rushed down the stairs, through the family room, the kitchen, the dining room, the living room, and into the foyer.

I stopped dead. My skin crawled.

The evening light was streaming through a frosted glass panel which now covered the entire top half of my front door. The light was golden-hued and I could see dust specks floating towards me. White wisps of smoke wafted towards the ceiling from the hinges. Embossed on the panel was a silhouetted figure of a man in profile, wearing a wide-brimmed hat, with his coat collar turned up and a pipe in his mouth. It was the same man, with a huge Adam's apple!

My front door did not have a glass panel. It was just a heavy mahogany door with brass fittings. So where did this come from? I pushed at the pane, but it was firmly installed and I could see strands of steel running through it. I hit it with the shovel, but it did not shatter or crack. There was not a single splinter or sliver of wood or shard of glass anywhere on the floor. The door remained as strong as before.

Must be some type of tempered glass, maybe even bullet proof. What magic is this?

I opened the door and ran out. There was nobody there. A cool breeze was blowing, bringing in a scent of pine needles and wild-flowers like fragrant cudweed. I stepped onto the lawn and saw that the hosta I had planted was mashed into the soil. So it couldn't have been a dream. I went into the house, wondering what to do with the door and the glass panel. Then I left it alone.

The story fascinated many of my friends who came by. Most didn't want to believe what I told them. That's natural! Some raised their eyebrows, some smirked, some laughed aloud, but they all agreed that I was improving every day as a storyteller.

A philosopher in our circle theorized that there were implausible things in this world and under the stars that we don't know about yet. "We must keep pondering."

"Leave the glass panel as it is; maybe it has magical powers to protect your home," one of them opined. "If you rub it, a genie might jump out to grant you boons!"

"Why tinker with the unknown?"said another friend. "It's a fanciful story, nevertheless!"

My wife suggested at one of the parties that I create a script for a short film based on the story. "You have the experience of making advertising shorts."

Everybody raised a toast and said, 'Cheers to that!'

The door and its frosted glass panel, thus, became a talking point in our friends' circle. My family, of course, knew it was bought at the flea market on Steeles Avenue. "Shhh..," I had told them. "Let it remain a mystery story..."

This all happened about four years ago, as I mentioned before. My front yard is now ablaze with colour in the spring and summer with a burning bush or *Euonymus alatus* as they are called, and some lovely hostas in front of the maple that is now surrounded with a red haze, so common in summer. The white hibiscus that I planted is a wonderful little tree ringed with bright orange marigold clusters.

My elegant backyard boasts a splendid lace bark elm, a rapidly growing tree. It's already soaring about 20 feet or so, with its many graceful branches and complements the two golden maple trees on either side. A weeping willow is still a baby and will be an attraction in the far corner. Nearby is a small pond, with cardinal flowers and pickerel weed. Beyond that lies the Humber woods, dark and mysterious. It's all very nice and pretty and I host frequent parties for my business clients and friends here.

However, I still don't know whose mangled body it was, with its shattered skull, that I buried deep under the elm sapling. I have never read or heard anything about a tall and slender man in a black overcoat and hat who has been reported missing. Of course, sometimes I wonder if it was a stocky man of medium build who was the intruder. The human mind hallucinates to insulate it from the paranoia that follows a violent incident.

Our brains are protective of our being and grim memories fade away or get twisted with time, don't they? Some things have just never happened... Like my donation of a shovel to a busy, suburban thrift store in another town; and some clothes that I shredded and turned into ash in a fire pit. And what about that pool of blood I washed away with acid on the marble tiles, near the splintered door of my home, on that horrid spring day?

The Nowhere Road

"Where are you headed, you people? How did you get here?" The farmer on the tractor squinted at us, the sun in his eyes. The tractor was painted in a strange mixture of beige and green colours that appeared to roll and ripple like waves. It looked like an all-terrain vehicle with some protrusions behind, which retracted when it stopped.

My boyfriend Greg and I had come out for a long weekend drive through scenic country roads, starting just after noon on Friday. There was nothing to do, nowhere to go, because of the COVID-19 lockdown and restrictions in Regina.

Around three hours into the drive, Greg suggested, 'Let's have a little adventure,' and veered onto a dusty grid road. We shouldn't have, because we saw no vehicles after driving for over an hour—no farmhouses; just the flat Boreal grassland plain.

We found ourselves at a fork on an unpaved, unnamed road; our GPS had gone silent, and we were lost. We reasoned we were somewhere east of Melfort in the Carrot River Valley after driving some 420 km north from home. We'd stocked up on food and had some jerrycans of fuel. The air was still all around us, dusk was falling and we could see the stars beginning to come out in clusters in the cloudless sky. We thought we would wait until dawn before trying to find our way to a main road. Greg was tired and I was always a little nervous in the dark.

The gentle warmth of the early morning sun greeted us, a comforting reminder that spring had arrived, as we groggily emerged from our curled-up sleeping positions on the car seats. We drank some tepid coffee, poured out from one of our thermos flasks.

"Well? Where you headed?' the farmer asked again, getting down from his tractor. He was good-looking, maybe 40 years or so, with blue jeans and a black and orange tartan shirt, sleeves pulled up to the elbows. A green beret perched askew on his head.

What a strange machine; have seen nothing like it...

"We came out for a drive, all the way from Regina, and we slept in our vehicle during the night," Greg said. "We are lost...Where are we now? Where do these roads lead to?"

"You are now in Somewhere." He laughed. "If you take the road that I am on...and you should take it...It will take you to Highway 3 and to Prince Albert. You can then be on proper roads or Highway 41 to Saskatoon and home..."

"Are you a farmer? We didn't see a farmhouse anywhere near, no barns, no silos, no cattle... And no people."

"Farmer, yes. Sometimes a farmer, sometimes a scout, mostly a head hunter." He laughed again.

"Okay, great joke," said Greg, also laughing. "But can you tell us where this fork goes?" He pointed to his left where the stretch of narrow dirt road went straight out like an arrow reaching to a point in the far distance.

The farmer stared at us, as if he was inspecting us, then shook his head. After a moment, he said, "That goes to nowhere... don't take it. Or maybe it leads to your Garden of Eden. It's your life, your choice. So many challenges... So many temptations!" He shrugged, turned his back on us, clambered onto his machine, pressed a switch, pulled a lever and chugged away.

I looked at Greg and saw that he was as baffled as I was by the farmer's strange comments. He glanced at me with raised eyebrows before starting the car.

Around us, beyond the junction, the soil was black as night.

Miles of barren ground, with patches of green and gold, that glowed brightly with the rising sun. No trees could be seen, although there was a shadow of thick woods on the horizon.

"If we are in the Carrot Valley area, those trees would be part of the Pasquia boreal forest. We can get proper maps from the park office there," I said.

"I think we should follow the farmer's direction and get onto the highway. We can get into a motel some place and be home by noon tomorrow," Greg said.

I was not one to give in, however. What the farmer said had shifted my attention to the woods in the distance. "Let us, at least, drive towards the woods and see what's there. We could turn around if we don't see any settlements."

I had read about pretty towns like Glasyln, Spiritwood, Shell Lake and many others in the region. There were even some ancient diamond mines mentioned. "Let's go," I prodded Greg, who seemed reluctant to drive into the unknown. "We have three big cans of gasoline as well for the drive."

The farmer and his tractor had disappeared, as we turned into the 'nowhere' road and set off. Greg, who drives big rigs across Saskatchewan and Manitoba, drove fast, our SUV hitting 80 to 100 km in stretches, the dust kicking up around us and leaving a hazy wake behind.

We must have driven for three hours or so, but the woods seemed as distant as it was when we got into the fork.

"Stop, Greg, stop," I shouted. "I think I saw a lion on the side of the road."

"What bosh! There are no lions here. You must have seen a moose or, maybe, even a bison. This is Saskatchewan, not Africa."

I rubbed my eyes. "I am sure I saw a lion. But stop anyway. I must be seeing things. I swear I saw a couple of giraffes too... Just a blur as we whizzed by."

A few minutes later, Greg said, "Liz... Liz. I can't stop the truck. The brakes are not working. Maybe the brake pads are gone..." There was now panic is his voice. "...And I can't control the steering. Liz, look, I have my foot off the accelerator and the car is still speeding...Wooo!" He kept pumping the brakes, but the car raced on. We felt trapped in a high-velocity wind tunnel—similar to those I had seen in some movies. The car seemed to stand still, with woods full of spruce, poplar and aspen, and prairie grasslands rushing away behind us. I screamed. I checked my watch and realized we had been caught up in this 'air tube' for over an hour. The watch then went dead. So did Greg's and the clock on the SUV dashboard. Our phone screens were black. My stomach churned. Greg grabbed my hand as if to reassure me, but I could see he was terrified, too.

Our vehicle screeched to a sudden halt, as if it had hit a wall of rubber. On our left was part of the woods we had seen from far away. On the right was what looked like a huge octagonal structure, less than a foot above the ground with several tiny chimneys puffing out pale blue smoke at intervals. The surrounding ground was overgrown with weeds and dying trees. A megalith sat amidst boulders and small broken rocks.

"Where and what is this place? Is this some sort of cremation ground? What is this smoke? Is there some power plant below us?" Greg looked worried. He tried to start the truck. Nothing. "The battery is dead, I think. Or the ignition is gone. If this is a cemetery or some kind of engineering station, there must be people around too. There must have been a small settlement or mining camp here long ago. I don't think it's on any map."

There was a sudden swirl of heavy crosswinds, and round and round our vehicle went, making 360 degree turns for what felt like an eternity and then sudden silence. We must have lost consciousness.

When we opened our eyes, we found ourselves on a mesa with steep sides. We didn't know how our SUV got up here. There were no roads visible; only a narrow winding track down the wooded side of the table top hill.

In the distance, we could see a small town, with round houses set in expanding rings with a bigger home or a palace in the middle. A blue-green glow or halo ringed the town. A lake shimmered far away, with blue waters and a sandy beach. Not a cloud was to be seen in the blue-domed sky above us. Around the town—on three sides— were thick woods. Beyond that, we could see only sand dunes.

"My God, I think we are in the dunes of the Great Sand Hills in the south-west of Saskatchewan," Greg was pointing to the town. "But we were heading north...We were in the north. How the fuck did we reach here? Something weird is happening, Liz, and how did we get to the top of this mountain?... What exactly did that farmer tell us?"

I was now in tears and terrified, thinking about what could happen next. "I don't seem to remember the farmer's exact words, except that he mentioned a garden."

Greg and I clambered down the steep hill to head into the town. It was an easy descent, the track winding through the woods with its canopy of trees, their rich, green leaves and thick branches overlapping each other. A cool breeze, rich in oxygen, wafted around us and although we couldn't see the sun, we saw a mellow golden hue bathing the town. The woods merged into the settlement, and I estimated it took about 30 minutes for us to reach the area.

As we approached, we saw cube-like carriages moving around, hovering silently over glass-tiled roads, within luminous markings. There were big crystal balls rolling along in the curb lanes. We saw people in the carriages and in the spinning globes. The roads came and went in all directions but seemed to converge at a distant point and disappear into the ground, in front of the palace-like structure, which had a glittering, spiral dome.

A tunnel, perhaps? Coming out from the other side of the town?

We moved a little closer and my heart skipped a beat. These were not people, but some kind of humanoids. None of them had a face. No hair, no eyes, no nose, no ears. Some of these creatures, dressed in silk-like gowns were gliding along on elevated, moving walkways. On a grassy lane, running alongside the walkways—and spaced well apart—strolled animals in a two-by-two formation—

elephants, lions, tigers, giraffes, wolves, dogs, cats, armadillos, zebras, alligators, horses and various types of cattle, many species of apes, reptiles and rodents. Swarms of insects and birds of many kinds and sizes floated over them, without any flapping of wings— as if they were riding some air current—making no sound. None of them had faces.

On the other side of the lane there was a huge trench with brilliant, blue flowing water and within it were fishes of many hues and sizes, several whales, dolphins, and scores of other aquatic creatures.

Multi-colored orchids, the size of small trees, edged the glass roads. Behind them, there were coconut groves and orchards thick with mango trees, apples, pears, and every other variety of fruit trees, vegetable gardens, vine yards and flower beds of all kinds between widely spaced houses, which had gilt-edged picture windows. Most of the houses were awash in an amber glow. Some creatures walked into or flew into these round structures, erected a little distance from the roads, walkways and trenches.

"Where are we, Greg? I am scared now. Are we in a dream? Shouldn't we go back? How do we get back home?"

Greg was, however, like a child at a fair, his eyes now wide with delight. "Not yet... Let us walk around. I don't think they can see or hear us. They don't look like they will hurt us."

Greg had this same look when we visited a miniature city some years ago in the town of Whitby, in Ontario. "We are seeing a kind of sci-fi here. I don't know if this is real, or it's because of that thing we smoked some hours ago. There is no motorized movement, no mechanical devices, no hum of any kind...What about food for these beings?...What do they do? There are no shops anywhere..."

Some humanoids, holding the hands of miniaturized versions of themselves, moved along another horizontal walkway towards some larger structures that emitted an indigo glow.

Those must be their children. Going to a school or an arcade?

"Hey," I called out.

Nobody responded. I stepped onto the road and a humanoid walked right through me. My body touched nothing. I moved to the middle of the road, although Greg tried to grab me, and stood in front of a carriage. The vehicle also passed through me—as if I didn't exist. I climbed onto the walkway, stepped on the grassy lane, and reached out to prod a baboon. I touched nothing.

I held Greg's hand, and I felt him grip mine.

Okay, I am not an ectoplasm. Are these creatures robots? Is this some sort of matter transference happening that is letting them and the cubes go through me?

As we wandered awestruck through the beautiful gardens and the orchards, one of the houses in that quadrant took on an alluring, green hue.

"It's calling us, Greg," I burst out and walked towards it. Something drew me towards it. I felt bewitched.

I touched the smooth outer wall. It went boom! A plume of fragrant smoke followed a tiny blast. My hand singed, and I saw with a sort of delighted horror that the middle finger of my right hand was now whole. I had lost the tip of the finger at the first joint in an accident when I was five years old. I had neither missed it nor been thinking of it until now. The mini explosion caused no pain, however, and there was no blood. The finger was complete. Some sort of instant healing, with no scarring.

Wow, look at my finger moving, complete with a new nail. What on earth is this place? What happened to my finger? Magnetic pulse therapy or surgery? Tissue rebuilding?

I rubbed my eyes and looked at the wall of the house. The structure was as it was before, beautiful with its oval windows and brilliant shingles in many colours. There were no marks on the wall.

"Touch nothing," Greg said. "Let's go towards the lake... There must be somebody—or something—that can explain all these strange things to us."

All around us, beings were moving in and out of various buildings. We could see the lake through the orchid trees and headed towards it. We didn't reach it, however. Four humanoids blocked and cushioned us on a walkway, steering us back to the green structure that had healed my finger. Some sort of scented mist descended as we entered a vestibule, and Greg and I were out cold.

We didn't know how many hours we were blanked out. When we woke up, we could hear the rumble of a storm approaching. We were in the open, sitting in our car, at the foot of the table top mountain that we were on a few hours ago or a few minutes ago...

Crosswinds similar to what hit us earlier in the day began swirling and turning, violently disturbing the atmosphere and spinning our vehicle again in circles. Round and round we went, and we held onto each other, our eyes shut, unable to do anything else.

Sudden silence followed and our vehicle engine was throbbing with its familiar hum. We were on the dusty road again and the woods were way behind us. The mesa had disappeared.

Greg gripped the steering wheel, let out a whoop, and drove at speed. "Whatever that was, whatever we saw, whatever we felt—that is done... We need to reach home. And do you know, Liz, the sciatica that was troubling me these past two years is gone... No pain at all. Who will believe what happened to us?"

"And... And my finger? Doesn't it look good now?... How?"

I looked at Greg. He looked much older, with lots of grey hair, all thinned out in the front and sides of the scalp. There were wrinkles on his forehead and he had bags of skin hanging under his eyes. "Something has happened, Greg. You look about 60 years old and what's with this baldness?"

I looked in the vanity mirror on the visor above the passenger seat. "Oh God," I screamed. "I am an old woman. This can't be, this can't be happening to me. That's not me..."

Weeping, I touched the wrinkles on my face and rubbed the gray hairs on my head. I had bulked up and my clothes were tight on my body, while Greg's shirt was hanging loose on his thin frame.

We had reached the same fork at the road we rested a few hours ago. Both of us felt a sense of *déjà vu...*

"I don't believe this. Look..." Greg said, pointing to the side of the road.

A farmer was riding a tractor, painted in brilliant beige and green colours, with several protuberances like big exhausts. He stopped by us, turning the machine towards the forked road where we had just come from.

Getting down, he called out, "Where you headed, you people?" The large tires were muddy and a film of dust coated the tractor. The farmer looked about 65 or 70 years old, with a long white beard lying flat on his black and orange tartan shirt, and flowing white hair at the back. A faded green beret was askew on his head. He was mocking us. "Hey, I have seen you somewhere... Wait, yes, it's the same machine... Must have travelled a long way, I am sure. The vehicle is all dusty. You could use a shower, right?"

I could see him smile as the golden evening sun seemed to shine a spotlight on him.

"Feeling rejuvenated? You are all cleaned up, you know. Both of you." He wiggled a finger at us. "You have been away from this world of yours for thirty-one years now."

"What... What?" Greg asked, trying to get out of the car.

"Wait," I said, tugging at his shirt. "He looks familiar, too. We saw somebody like him on a newer tractor of this same colour when we came here yesterday or this morning—at this very junction."

The farmer stepped forward. "Thirty-one years now... You won't... I remember, yes. Here, same place." He was laughing now.

I stepped out of the car, along with Greg. "We must have seen his son, clean shaven, yesterday on a tractor...With the same fittings behind it...," I said. "And he was also wearing a green cap like this one...and... Do you have a son, sir? We think we met him yesterday."

"Na, na," his shook his head. "No son here... I can change the way I look whenever I want... I can turn into a horse, giraffe, lion or even a small dragonfly. I can also speak umpteen languages."

He caressed his beard. "Let me tell you a secret. We have cloned you... Like many others and the beautiful creatures of your world. For the greater good of the universe and its many galaxies. You have been living for thirty-one delightful years in a stealth dome, invisible even to your most powerful satellites."

Greg and I looked at each other. "Deranged," Greg whispered. "He is somebody else, not the same guy... I think we're hallucinating ... About something... Somewhere. Let's go."

The farmer's voice took on a rhythmic cadence. "Sorry about your two children, though. We needed to send them away with your reproductions. They are now grown up, happy and thriving."

"Children? What children? Send them away where?" I yelled.

"We put your clones and your children, a son and a daughter, into hibernation pods that were teleported into the cosmos. It's a journey of two earth years through deep space. Everything will be fine with you. Your world and life will be the same as before, if not better.

"The Caesarian marks on your stomach vanished long ago, Liz. We had to operate, you know, your pelvis was too narrow for childbirth... Oh, that was so many years ago. But I assure you, your children are exciting assets in our world. Their IQ is almost 900, not like the miniscule average of 100 for humans on this planet. Also, we have long life-spans, much like the legends of Methuselah or Jared in your religious book. All of us are empaths and telepaths, and we have several ways of sensory communication, many of which are still unknown in your world."

Greg and I were now looking at him, our mouths open in shock.

"Both of you have been outstanding samples and have done good work during the past three decades. Liz, you marshalled the resources allocated to you, especially the penguin colony so well—and, the pygmies of the Congo, children of the Aguaruna people from the Amazon and the Sentinels from the Andamans. Just amazing."

"You are lying," I said. "We turned back because we were trapped in a storm about four hours from here." I turned to Greg. "Was it today or yesterday?... We saw strange things... humanoids."

The farmer continued, "Oh, yes, the flamingoes too. Kudos to you, Greg. Your recreated a version of Kenya's Lake Nakuru that was perfect in every detail. The crocodiles and the dolphins also took a special liking to you, I heard. The original flamingoes have already returned to Kenya, the penguins to Antarctica, the crocs to Madagascar and the dolphins to their many oceans. You were exemplary executives at the recreation and art centres, and you were popular raconteurs, playing a leadership role among trainers in the indigo buildings... Your clones are like the humanoids that you saw."

"What about the storm?" I asked again.

"The geomagnetic storm was a type of transport vehicle." The farmer paused. "However, now that your job with us is done, you are free to go."

"Free to go?"

"Yes, you were part of our last batch of volunteers."

"Volunteers?" My head was spinning. This was all too much for my addled brain.

"Yes, we gave you the choice—about the road to choose at this fork many years ago." He spread out his hands. "You chose us and we chose you."

"What about this?" I asked, pointing to my finger.

"Oh, we repaired that as part of the cloning process. The structure you touched was primed for your stay—the embedded dynamic codes have healing and reconstructive properties. We studied your lizards and salamanders. And Greg's sciatica is gone too. There is so much in your world that you choose to ignore. I must say, however, you enjoyed living in that Trulli-style home all these years with your children and others in the community."

Greg interrupted him. "What about that octagonal building and the mesa and that... That magical city we saw?"

The farmer looked at us affectionately, his eyes drooping a little, a smile crinkling the corners of his mouth. "Okay, since you have been brilliant partners with us, I think you deserve an explanation, although I don't need to give you one." He looked up at the sky, and then back at us. "We require species from this world for regenerating and populating one of our new planets. You have fine specimens of flora and fauna, birds, insects, subterranean creatures, your waters and mountains and millions of years of memories that will assist us.

"Eons ago, we replicated your dinosaurs, the dodo, the sabre-toothed cat, woolly mammoth, giant moa, millions of insects and plant species that are extinct here...They are flourishing in their natural surroundings out there. You, Liz, you have 28 trillion cells in your body and Greg has 36 trillion. The transfer of cells is a delicate affair and we had to let all clones adapt to our troposphere, before teleporting them. That does take some time. But we do not harm any worlds or any beings... The octagon you saw houses numerous galactic pods and the mesa is a cloak over our main launch vehicle. We are now winding down our 80-year earth mission..."

He leaned towards Greg. "You must have heard of alternate universes and wormholes, right? There are different planes of existence where time and space are not according to what you perceive. Sometimes, a minute for you may be many years in some places."

He was staring at us, a sort of hypnotic gaze. "Your world will learn about four-dimensional continuum, entanglement physics and the capabilities of subatomic particles in due course. In your instance, we tweaked and froze time for many years—for both of you and all people in your circle and rewrote memories. We also corrected and refined your genetic codes, making you immune to many diseases. You will lead healthy lives and have two fine children. Everything, however, is just a concept... Illusion, really! "

The farmer extended a hand and seemed to pluck something from the air. "Here, keep this. A little gift from us; you will, however, remember it as an inheritance from your grandmother."

He handed me two small, teal-coloured, ping-pong sized balls. They were soft to the touch, like silk, but a little heavy. "They are timed to open exactly after 36 hours of your time."

A green flare flashed in the distance. "It's time to go; yes time!" The farmer chuckled. His hands were moving in small circles in front of us. "Enjoy your life. Your cortex memories of the past thirty-one years in our earth capsule and whatever I told you will now begin to fade away... In a slow way, in about two days..."

Greg shook his head. "I don't believe a word of what you are saying... Why are you telling us these stories if you are going to erase our memories—of what you call our happy times?"

"That's the law of the universe, my friend. Our Swing-Swirl Protocol demands that, if requested, we inform you about the past... At some future date, you might decide to recollect scattered fragments of your life or get enlightened..."

"Enlightened...? What does that...?"

The farmer snapped his fingers. "We will be back, though... Not in your lifetime, of course. Maybe in another 1,000 or 2,000 years or so, depending on how your species and civilization develop. It might be your descendants who will come to visit your world. Our home is in one of the spiral arms of the Triangulum Galaxy. It's a long way away, through a black hole Accretion Disk and much further than the Magellanic Clouds. So, it's goodbye, for now."

The farmer tapped both sides of his head with his fingers.

"Look, look... He is changing." I grabbed hold of Greg's arms.

The transformation was quick; his moustache and beard disappeared, and he was a young man again. The beret was gone, and his bald head glistened in the gloom.

As his nose, eyes, and ears dissolved, he took on a brownish-pinkish colour. His tartan shirt and jeans had given way to a gown. Climbing onto the tractor, he flicked a switch. The machine pulsated, changed into a crystal cube and took off like a bullet, becoming a dot in the distance, and disappearing into the horizon.

I fiddled with one of the little ping-ping orbs the farmer had given us. There was no opening of any kind. "Throw it on the ground. Let's see if it breaks," Greg said.

The object bounced back with a hum into my hand like a rubber ball. I threw it again, harder. It bounced back again. Greg threw the other one as high and as far as he could. The little ball was like a boomerang. After a few seconds, it zoomed in with a loud hum into his hand. "Wow!" Greg exclaimed.

I felt my stomach. I couldn't feel any scar of an operation. "We had children?...I had two C-sections?" My head was now in a swirl and I fainted.

When I came to, Greg was cuddling me and cooing in my ear. "It's okay, baby. It's all okay. We are safe. We gotta go home."

We got into the SUV, turned onto the open road and raced towards Highway 3 and Prince Albert. We then reached Highway 41 and literally flew in the gathering darkness towards Saskatoon and onto Regina. Traffic was light and we reached home a little after midnight. On the way, our faces and bodies changed; Greg was again the handsome 26-year-old man I am so much in love with. He held me close at one of the rest stops. "Oh God, you are my lovely Lisa again. Look at your eyes. Oh God!' He caressed my stomach and my breasts, and all my fears and confusion melted away.

I am at my doctors's office to show him my finger. He gives me a puzzled look. "What about it?"

"You know I had a finger with the top part gone...Why is it like this today, all good?"

"What do you mean?... It has always been like this, ever since you registered at this office. I don't recollect having seen any chopped finger on you... Is this some kind of joke?"

I didn't know how to explain the events of the day before. I can only recollect a dream of dust and brilliant lights flashing... And then ... Then nothing. Greg is also full of doubt and can't summon up anything, except seeing a young farmer on a tractor at a fork on an interior road. He remembers the farmer, because there was a sapling on the back seat of our SUV. "The farmer left it," Greg said, sounding absent-minded.

I found two strange little balls in my handbag and did not know how they got there. They were of a pretty colour and great texture, so I kept them. However, they each opened like a lotus on Tuesday morning. Nestled inside each pot, on a soft piece of blue satin, was what looked like a diamond.

"What is this? Could this be real?" I asked Greg, who took one out and turned it between his fingers. The stone glowed, the many cut faces shimmering and sparkling with white light and flashes of blazing red.

"The farmer gave them to us," Greg said. "Why? We just went out for a long drive and met him at the fork... And then we came back... Can't remember anything he said to us."

"Let us go downtown, there are many jewellers in the Victoria Avenue and Ring Road areas. Let's check it out."

This is a morning of ecstasy. The first jeweller we visited looked at one of the stones with a monocular loupe to his eye and gasped. "This is real... It's an original cut. Never seen anything like this before... Now, you be careful with this... This should be in a solid safe in a vault. How did you get this?"

"It's a family heirloom," I said. "It's been with my family for ages... A couple of generations."

The jeweller said, "You know, this is a red, round cut, Type II diamond. Very rare. It's a stunning stone. Offhand, I would say it's worth around two million dollars or more... I can help you sell or auction this. You can get much more then!"

Greg gulped, squeezing my hand.

"No, no," I said. "We are not selling. We just... We just wanted to know its approximate worth."

"Let us talk, let us talk," the jeweller said, holding Greg's hand and not wanting to let us leave. He walked us to the shuttered door to let us out. "Come back any time. Call me, it's my private number. Talk to your lawyer as well. Don't let it attract attention." He handed me a silver-gilded card.

"Okay, okay, we will think about it and contact you," I said.

"Let's get the stones into a bank vault," Greg said, after we got into our SUV. "The other one must also be worth this much. This money should give us a roaring start. We could open a big trucking company. I won't have to drive big rigs for others anymore. But why did the farmer give... The farmer... Farmer, which farmer? Farmer?... What am I talking about?"

"I think it's the excitement, baby. Both of us have been babbling about some farmer these past two days. These stones have been in my family for ages. I told you about them before."

In the evening, we drove to my parents' home in Moosejaw and I showed them the stones. "Do you know how much these are worth? I asked my dad. "They are real diamonds... rare diamonds."

Dad shrugged his shoulders. "Yes, we know. Worth millions, right? Your grandmother got them from her grandfather, who was a prospector in the Gahcho Kué mines area, in today's Northwest Territories. They were gifted by a chief from the First Nations of the Akaitcho Treaty 8 Territory and then your great-great grandfather got it cut somewhere. Those were marvellous stories that we have heard from your grandma, bless her soul. I think the authentication and ownership papers are in the bank."

Mom didn't find it amusing."Why are you carrying them around?" she asked. "Grandma gave them to you on your 18th birthday. You agreed to keep them in the vault..."

Then there is the matter of the sapling we found in the back seat of our SUV.

Wonder who kept the plant in the vehicle? Must be some prank, but an expensive prank, nevertheless.

What we thought was a sapling is an exquisite bonsai tree, its roots encased in a polished mahogany box. The 24-inch gnarled tree is heavy with tiny, golden mangoes, hanging in clusters, amid bright green leaves, with three blood-red fruits at the top, like stars on a Christmas tree. On the base of the box is a golden plaque with luminescent words moving like subtitles on a cinema screen, in a loop. There is no battery or a power source anywhere on the box.

The quixotic message reads, "The fruits of this tree contain your life force. You can eat the yellow fruits...They will regenerate every day and keep you radiant and happy. However, pluck not and eat not the red fruits at the top, the sweetest of them all. If you eat even one of them, both of you will mentally age 31 years, and a flood of disjointed, disturbing, and melancholic memories of a different world will overwhelm you. It's your choice, your fork on the road..."

Is That You, Rebecca?

"Rebecca," he shouted. Or was it 'Erica'? Old Johnny was in a grumpy mood.

The ambulance crossed the West Mall and Queensway intersection and turned north, picking up speed.

"Is that my girl over there? Tell her to get over here. Whom is she talking to?" he shouted again. There were occasional bursts of conversation on the ambulance walkie-talkie, above the hum of the engine and a distant sound of road traffic.

"Ah, we are on the Agawa Canyon Train," Johnny mumbled. "This is a fun ride. We used to ride on this train. Yes, more than 60 years ago. We cuddled and kissed, and I became as hard as the granite of the King Mountain in the Algoma Highlands. Do you remember that, Rebecca, eh? Awesome, awesome! Are you listening?"

The paramedic who was driving the ambulance laughed. "Listen," he told his partner. "Old Johnny is horny, as usual."

"Can't hear him clearly... What's his story?" his partner, who had only recently joined the service, asked.

"It sounds like a disjointed jumble of words, but he is clear about things. We once recorded his murmurings and played it back slow. It was fascinating, I must say. Gave all of us an idea of his younger days. We are all very fond of the old-timer. He is quite harmless."

"Oh, I could see that in the hospital," his partner said, looking back at the stretcher through the glass divider. "Nurses and doctors all seemed to know him well and were so solicitous."

"Yes mate, you will come across many such people now that you are in the service. Oh, this traffic... And people just don't give way to emergency vehicles. It's a real problem. Look at this guy cutting in front of us." He hooted his horn once and switched on a short burst of the siren.

"Heh, heh, heh, there goes the train whistle," Old Johnny called out. "Whoo, hoo!"

Potholes on the road made the ride a bit bumpy. Old Johnny chuckled, as he bounced up and down. "Oh, Rebecca, oh Rebecca, oh. And in the Agawa River, do you remember, Rebecca? We waddled in and saw otters making love, twisting and turning and you wanted to do the same?"

His words were now coming out in a rush. "And we sure did. Yes, we sure did, down by the bank of the stream, on the grass, under the hot sun," Old Johnny was ecstatic. "We saw two children watching from behind a bush and we shouted at them, 'Shoo, shoo, go away'. Like this, like this." Johnny wiggled his fingers.

The ambulance driver laughed. "We have heard this before. Here it comes, his romantic interludes. Incoherent, but he tells a great story. It's sad, really. Nobody has the time to listen to him."

He got the ambulance into the middle lane as the traffic crawled. "We can't use the siren unless we are rushing to a hospital or trauma centre. Here, we are taking Johnny to his group home. So there is no hurry, anyway."

Old Johnny's voice had now gone up a notch to compensate for the road noise. "We walked along the Chapleau Trail, and oh my god, it had so many ancient trees. Maple and oak and aspen. The beams of sunlight were poking through the foliage, making the leaves all gold and green and creating cool shadows on the edges. Then you wanted to walk barefoot and then tried to ride on my back. Have you forgotten?" His voice trailed away with a deep sigh.

Old Johnny was now silent.

"Should we stop and check up on him?" the rookie paramedic asked, looking back again through the window behind him. "Why has he stopped talking?"

"It's okay," said the driver. "He is reliving, trying to remember things. We have seen this before. Then comes a jumble of words."

"Your eyes are beautiful, Rebecca. Remember how I kissed

them?" Old Johnny puckered his lips, blowing wet kisses into the air. "Squirrels? Oh yes, there were hundreds of them around. And chipmunks. You laughed when I chased those squirrels, running after them like this." Old Johnny was now flailing his legs about. Running, running. "The squirrels scampered up the trees, like this, like this."

The vehicle was now on Highway 427 and sped northward. The driver sounded the horn again as he crossed lanes along with a blare of the siren. The disconnected, but pulsating female voice of a 911 dispatcher asking for an ambulance to reach an accident site in Caledon floated through the vehicle.

"Where are you, Rebecca? I can hear you talking. Whom are you talking to?" Johnny's voice was high-pitched. "Who is that man over there with you? Are you wearing your yellow floral skirt?"

There were orange curtains across the side windows, and Johnny couldn't look out. He craned his neck, trying to see the driver's cab. He couldn't see anything, and his neck ached.

Old Johnny was angry now. His hands had become fists, and he was trembling. "Get over here, Rebecca, get over here. I want you here. Are you flirting with someone?" He wheezed as he tried to regain his breath.

"Rebecca, you did this to me on Moonlight Beach at Ramsey Lake, remember? On the paddle boat, you ignored me...And I kept asking you for a kiss. I begged and pleaded. I said come close, come to me and you didn't. You were there on the boat, weren't you? No? Heh, heh, heh, no, it wasn't you... Maybe it was Sandy."

The driver changed four lanes as he prepared to take the exit ramp. He said, "Old Johnny is upset because he can't see us. He always wants to see people and have people around him..."

"Yeah, I thought so, judging by his non-stop chatter."

'You know we have to restrain people like Johnny; he hates that. He is fond of pushing and pulling things... And you know the kind of sensitive equipment we have on board. There are many residents at the home who demand vehicles like TransHelp, but we can't help them there. They have to be transported in an ambulance, that is the rule. Of course, we can push open the bulkhead partition—this panel behind you—if the need arises or if we want to attend to them. You know about it..."

"How is his interaction with other residents and staff?"

The driver said, "They all like him. But he reserves his attention only for female clients and staff. You can see the welcome Johnny will get once we reach his long-term care home in North York. He has been in hospital with bronchitis for three weeks now, and everybody misses him."

"You like this run, do you? I mean, it's not active duty—this ferrying of people to and from long-term care homes."

The driver nodded. "I have been working for over 26 years, buddy. Sick of rushing to road crashes and picking up squashed and smashed victims and body parts from cars and from the asphalt. It gets to you bad. I have told the dispatchers to mark me for this type of job. There is no tension and I know residents of these homes."

He slowed down, took a turn to the right at the 427 and Major Mackenzie Drive intersection and crept eastward.

Old Johnny muttered something about being in a nickel mine elevator in Sudbury. Cool darkness, all around, with only the dim yellow lights throwing shadows on the cavern walls. "Slow, slow, Rebecca...slow slow," his tone was relaxed as the words floated away. "Ozo, Ozo." he shouted.

"Whenever a new nurse or staff member joins the home, they think he is uttering gibberish the whole day," the driver said. "Now, listen carefully, he is mumbling 'Osha, Osha or Ozo, Ozo'. What he is saying is 'Awesome, awesome'.."

"Has he no family? What about his wife, children?"

"Yes, Janet, that was his wife's name. She has passed on...Gone about eight years ago, I think. He had a daughter, Grace, who used to visit him once a month, although Johnny couldn't recognize her. She died about a year ago. Cancer, pancreatic. They have little chance, you know. Grace was only about fifty-six or so."

"This is really interesting and a little sad. Tell me more."

"Yes, it was Grace who brought him to the home six years ago—he was losing his memory by then and she couldn't manage him. She was a frail and sickly woman who had not married and had nobody to help her. Apparently, Old Johnny had a tendency to wander off and required police intervention when he went missing. They would find him in another part of the town, sitting on some mall bench or loitering in shops selling women's clothes and lingerie. Funny guy, I have heard that he loved standing in front of mannequins that are dressed in skirts or undergarments."

"Real horny guy, right?"

The driver said, "Old Johnny doesn't remember much. He is about eighty-five, and is taken to Sherway Hospital every three months or so. He has this chronic lung problem, besides other ailments like osteoarthritis and some kidney issues."

"Lung problems are the worst in the long-term care homes, I have heard," his partner said. "I am sure residents with personalities like Johnny can lighten up the atmosphere. In fact, Johnny's story should be part of our curriculum—shows us how to deal with frail people with various behavioral issues, not just emergency care alone."

"He still has behavioural issues. He did try to get away from the home on two occasions after throwing tantrums. The first one, staff found him on a bus headed to North York; nobody knew from where he got the money for the fare. The second time, he reached the gate and had to be carried forcibly into the home."

"Oh, that's terrible. From what I hear, I think he is the type of person who attracts compassion, especially from the maternal types."

"I agree," said the driver. "You know, Johnny is quite a star at the group home. If he hears a woman's voice, he thinks it's some woman he knew a long time ago. That sets off his imagination. It's like a spark plug that flickers and flashes through old memories. On some days, it could be Maria. On other days it's Sandra or June, or Alice and he calls out to them. Today it's Rebecca's day. He gets all aroused and then has to be strapped onto his bed. He keeps on making passes at the female staff and then squirms in delight."

The driver laughed out aloud. "One evening, Old Johnny grabbed the titties of Alicia Jones, the home administrator. She has big boobs, by the way. It took about 15 minutes to wrest his hands away from an embarrassed Mrs. Jones. She had to first sit and then lie down on his bed to stop him from hurting her. And all the while, Johnny was oohing and ahhing in delight."

The driver could not stop laughing. "And another day, we had a visiting nurse called Angela something. She was a new immigrant from the Philippines, and Johnny put his hand up her skirt, held on to her panties and just wouldn't let go. That was quite a struggle… Oh…and Angela refused to come to the home again."

"He must have been a real wolf in his days," the rookie said, looking back at Old Johnny through the window.

"He is still a good-looking man, Old Johnny," the driver nodded. "Word was that some of the female residents in the home were asking each other why Johnny didn't grab them by their titties! You know, after the Mrs. Jones incident…"

The Global Positioning System (GPS) mounted on the dashboard of the ambulance droned again. The recorded female voice was seductive and suggestive. "Take a turn to the left, ten metres, then turn right after twenty metres. Your destination will be on the left. You have arrived."

Lying on his stretcher, his arms secured by leather straps, Old Johnny wriggled like a worm on a hook and giggled. "Oh, Rebecca, I can hear youuuuu...oh Rebecca, ooh..." His voice then dropped to a whisper. "But didn't I strangle and drown you in Ramsey Lake that evening when the mist rose around us and I was hot and you were cold? Ooh, Rebecca, ooh..."

A Mugging

"My God, what happened to you?" my wife Marina screamed as I rushed into our house after she opened the door.

I must have been a sight. My arm in a make-shift sling, hair matted with blood, my left eye half shut, bruises on my cheek, my nose broken...

"Where were you? Why are you so late? What happened?" Marina was hysterical and almost in tears.

"Someone mugged me," I told her. "I got off the bus at Cloverdale station and was walking down Green Street. You know how dark that road is because of the enormous maple trees."

I touched a big, bloody bump on the back of my head.

"I had no chance. This guy jumped me from the shadows and he had some sort of metal baton with a knob at the end... And by God, he knew how to use it."

"But you have your watch on you wrist and your gold bracelet... Did he take your wallet? How much money did you have?"

"I don't know, I don't know. He took nothing... Just beat me up and kept hitting me after I fell. Then he ran away," I mumbled, as I limped to the washroom. "I need to take some painkillers."

I looked into the mirror...What a gruesome sight! How on earth could I explain to my darling little wife that I was the mugger on that dark and leafy Green St. and I was beaten to a pulp by my prey?

Ouch!

A Forced Checkmate

The raucous buzz of the cell phone pierced my ears and disturbed the sleep centre of my brain. I was in an enchanting dream state when the ringtone turned into the sound of a steam engine horn. Disoriented, and jerking my comforter away, I picked up the phone from the side table and said, 'Hello.'

The alarm clock said 4:20 am.

It was a Monday morning, May 20, 2024.

My wife Audrey was asleep in another bedroom. Audrey is a small-time actress, doing C-grade films for subscription-based cable TV and doing mono-acts in nightclubs. We have not been on good terms for over two years now and keep away from each other as much as possible. I detest her and the jobs she does. We do not have any children—after six years of marriage. Audrey once terminated a pregnancy, saying she didn't want childbirth to affect the shape of her body. She has cheated on me many times and has been pestering me for divorce, but I have refused to sign the papers. I don't want to give her half my wealth and half the value of our house.

A divorce or any formal separation would also damage my reputation. Currently, I am the preferred candidate in my riding for a seat in the Saskatchewan Legislative Assembly for the next election and any scandal could hurt my prospects. There is also a ministerial berth waiting for me. Audrey, such a repulsive creature, knows this and her monetary demands are now becoming unreasonable; and she knows that she has a cuckold for a husband.

"Mr. Jacob Slater?" The voice on the other end was tentative.

"Yes, who is this? At this time?"

"This is Terrence Logan from the Crisis Team, Regina Police South District. Sorry to call at this time of the morning; but I am afraid there has been a tragic incident and we would like to speak with you. It's urgent."

Incident? My wife is in her room. Oh shit, has anything happened to Joseph or Olivia?

"We believe Olivia is your sister. We found your number on her cellphone. Maybe, it would be better if you could come to her apartment as soon as possible. We are all here."

"What has happened to her, officer?" I asked. "I met her just four days ago and she was fine. Is she okay and... And her daughter?"

"Please come here. We have already informed your brother, Mr. Joseph Slater, as well," the officer said and hung up.

Wide awake now, I put on my trousers, a T-shirt and a jacket. Racing into the kitchen, I left a note for Audrey, saying the police were at Olivia's home and had summoned me there. I took my car key from the foyer, entered the garage, got into the car and hit the accelerator. It's a 15 minute drive to reach her place.

I hope everything is okay with her. She is an impractical woman, but she is still my sister.

"Hey, Jos," I called my brother, using the voice-activated dashboard device. "The police just called me about an incident concerning Olivia. Where are you?"

"Yeah, they called me too. I am on the way and almost at the apartment," he said. "I don't know what this is about."

Olivia made bad decisions all her life and lives in a grubby apartment in a crumbling building in Dunford South, one of the poorest and high-crime areas in the city.

We sympathize with her, but she does not want any help from us. Her stubborn response is always, 'Ah, we are okay, guys, we will get by;' or 'Mind your own business, guys;' or 'We don't need your money or sympathy, okay?'

Olivia was only 18 when she married a slob named Gabriel, a loafer who hates work. A warehouse worker with idiotic muscles and weird tattoos, he charmed her with his trash talk. Our family was against the union, but Olivia was adamant and got her way. Dropping out of school after marriage, she took up odd jobs in coffee shops, supermarkets and warehouses or as a cleaner and scrounged around in thrift shops for clothes and utensils.

Three years ago, Gabriel had an accident at work; he said he fell into a drain or something and injured a foot.

'You don't have to come to the hospital, okay...' Olivia told us. 'Gab doesn't want to see you, okay?'

With disability cash from the government, he spends time in cheap bars or smoking weed. He gives no money at home and Olivia has to look after Keira, their five-year-old daughter.

Our parents have passed on while we got on with our lives. I live in a pleasant neighbourhood in Wascana View while Joseph, who is a little higher on the societal scale, lives in Arcola East. Both of us have government jobs; Joseph works for a federal agency, while I am with a provincial service department. As mentioned earlier, I am also a community activist and am getting ready to enter politics. Joseph is lucky, however, in his personal life. His wife Linda is a veterinary doctor with a flourishing practice and they have two bright children, Jackson and Joanne.

The time was just after 5.00 am and still dark when I reached the cluster of dilapidated brown-bricked apartment complex, where Olivia lived. Police 'crime scene' tape ringed the area around two buildings. Police officers were milling about and the grounds were awash with floodlights. Despite the chill of late March, gawkers had emerged from the neighbouring buildings and were crowding around the periphery of the block.

Parking the car on the road, I stepped onto a walkway littered with broken garbage bags, empty vodka bottles, and oily rags and hurried to Olivia's building. Identifying myself to a couple of officers at the entrance, I asked for Officer Logan.

I waited awhile, until the officer came down the elevator and said, "Come, your brother is already here." The elevator creaked as we rode to the eighth floor and Logan said, "Now, keep calm, Mr. Slater. We are still investigating the incident, but prima facie, we think there has been a murder-suicide in the apartment."

My heart seemed to stop, my mouth was dry and my head throbbed. What could I say? "Who...Who? Is Keira their daughter, okay? Is Olivia okay?"

Officer Logan did not look at me. He shook his head. "No, both the parents are gone. The child is safe and is now with one of the neighbours."

As I said before, Olivia was a scrounger, but avoided asking us for help. The three of us, however, have been meeting at a restaurant — nothing fancy—every month for the past two year. We meet, talk about old times, eat and go away. Every meeting is the same. We pick different items from the menu, Joseph and I ordering a dish each along with a salad and mashed potato, while Olivia orders four or five dishes. "I am hungry," she always said.

We keep rotating the way we pay. That is fine, but it was irritating to see that Olivia left most of the food on the table untouched and then tells the waiter 'Please doggy bag all this.' She turns towards us and says, "Oh, Gabs and Keira will love this."

This was not a one-off thing. She did this every month. Joseph also found this behavior exasperating, especially when it was her turn to play host. She tells us she didn't bring her credit card and doesn't have much cash on her. She orders one dish and so Joseph and I ask for a simple sandwich and coffee.

Saturday afternoon, May 18, 2024, I was in a foul mood after another bitter squabble with Audrey. It was then that Olivia called to say she can't make it for our usual restaurant rendezvous. It was her turn to play host.

This whole restaurant thing is getting irritating. We need to put an end to it. There is no reason to meet like this...

"Can you get us some food, Jeb? I don't feel well to come out to-day. Just buzz the intercom when you get here and I will come down and get it. Bring anything you want."

I heard Olivia sniffle.

Was that bastard husband of hers beating her and little Keira?

I said, "OK, I will get some Chinese food now, and will come by your apartment in the evening. I will bring a chocolate cake for Keira and a bottle of sweet wine for you. You may have to warm the food later..."

What a useless woman. What should we do with her?

Jos and I walked the full length of the corridor, with its broken and faded laminate, to Olivia's corner apartment. There were two officers standing outside the shattered door. The stench was terrible. Officer Logan handed some scented masks to us. "You will need these."

The officers ushered us into the living room. Joseph and I gagged. There was vomit and blood around the room. Olivia was on the floor, her limbs askew on the tacky rug in front of a shabby sofa.

Men and women in white gowns were taking photographs and looking at nooks and corners with torches and tongs, and officers kept coming and going out.

"The neighbours called the police at around 11:00 pm last night to report a child screaming in the apartment," Logan said. "The front door had been locked from the inside. We smashed the door to get in. The couple died, we think, sometime late on Saturday night and the little girl was alone in here the whole of yesterday."

"Come," he said, leading us into the cramped bathroom. Gabriel was lying there, without a shirt, his head half-submerged in the toilet bowl. The tattoo of a naked woman on his back had blackened and his skin sagged over the elastic band of his shorts.

"It looks like both suffered a lot," the officer said. "We will know what really happened only after the post-mortems and after our forensic teams complete their examination. It looks like food poisoning... See the half-eaten food all over the table and sofa. Now that you have identified the bodies, you can go home. There is no point in you both staying here. Come, I will take you to see the daughter."

The officer led us to an apartment midway down the corridor and knocked. A grey-haired woman opened the door, holding little Keira's hand. The child rushed out to hug me and cried out, "Uncle Jeb, uncle Jeb." I held her tight, patting her head, and Jos held one of her hands.

Office Logan tapped me on my shoulder and said, "I will call both of you, after we get the preliminary reports. One of you can take the child with you. She could not tell us anything, except that her mommy and daddy were both screaming."

Joseph and I walked down the stairs. He was almost in tears. "What could have happened? That Logan said it was a murder-suicide. Poison? Do you think Gabs did it? He was a slob, happy with his bottle. But murder? Was it Olivia? But why? "

We nodded to a couple of officers and walked towards our cars.

One of the gawkers approached us."Hey, what's happened up there... Any ideas? They didn't kill the girl, eh?"

"How many died in there, and who are you?" another ghoul asked, blocking my way. "Is it a boyfriend issue? Was there a rape involved?" He was licking his lips.

Rage rose within me like a coiled serpent. I turned around, bunched up my right fist and would have hit him if Jos had not held my hand. Muttering an expletive, I walked away. One of the officers, who was standing on the pavement, said, "Calm down, buddy... There will be more questions from many people."

Jos said, "I think I will take Keira home for now. I am sure Audrey wouldn't like her at your place. She hates kids."

Tuesday, May 21. I was in the office, handling routine files, my mind heavy with the images of Olivia and Gabriel, their bodies lying in the apartment. Poor souls. I was also talking to a lawyer about the formalities needed to adopt little Keira.

I can give Keira a decent life. But what happened in there? It must have been Gabs, the scoundrel. He must have killed Olivia...

A call from Officer Logan interrupted my work. "Mr. Slater, can you come by the police station at around 11:00 am tomorrow? I have also asked your brother to be present. We have some information on the deaths of your sister and her husband."

"Officer, do you have any idea when they will release the bodies, so that we can make the funeral arrangements?"

"That will take more than a week, Mr. Slater. Investigations are still ongoing. Anyway, be here at 11 tomorrow."

Wednesday, May 22. Jos and I reached the police station at almost the same time the next day. We waited for about 20 minutes for Logan to call us in. We were escorted into a room, which had a steel table and steel chairs and a small window with a view of only a brick wall. Logan closed the door and sat across us. A CCTV camera with a twinkling red light was pointed at us.

"I was busy with some officers; a briefing is still going on." He must have noticed our flustered faces and said, "Sorry for bringing you into this interrogation room. You should have no objection to our interview being recorded. There's nothing to worry about. It's normal procedure."

Joseph looked at me. I shrugged my shoulders.

"Okay, here goes. The medical examiner's report has come in. I can't give it to you now, but this is the gist. Gabriel Calado and Olivia Calado, husband and wife, died from poisoning. Traces of a banned pesticide were present in their viscera—administered through wine... The sediment, or the dregs at the bottom of a bottle of port that we found on the floor was loaded with pesticide."

"My God," I said, stifling the scream that rose in my throat.

"Holy hell," said Jos, holding his head in his hands. "It can't be... I never thought..."

"What is it?" Logan asked. "Is there something I need to know about?'

"I told you officer, I met Olivia last Saturday evening. That was on the 18th of May," I said. "I told you about it when you called me on Monday... about the incident with the shocking news."

"Yes, I remember. Go on..."

"We have never been to her apartment. I mean, both Jos and me. She didn't want us to go up there. That evening, we were to meet up in a restaurant, when she called me at around noon or so, saying she won't be coming and instead, asked if I could get her some food.

"I ordered some Chinese dishes, sweet and sour chicken...she likes that a lot... Noodles and beef strips in orange sauce. I also brought a chocolate cake and a bottle of sweet wine, a tawny port. I went to the building at—it must have been 5:30 pm or 6:00 pm— and buzzed her apartment. She came down and took the packages. She didn't want to talk. I asked her if she wanted some cash. She just shook her head and said, 'Thanks, Jeb. We are okay,' and then rushed back into the building lobby."

Logan was scribbling away on a note pad. He looked up at Joseph and said. "Anything on your mind, Mr. Slater?"

"No, nothing," Jos said. "I mean, you mentioned the bottle of wine... You see, the three of us, we all love this same wine. In our childhood days, it was a sort of tradition every Saturday. We were allowed to taste a wee bit of this wine, and we still continue to drink them. They are so chocolaty...I gave her a bottle of wine last week."

"So all three of you drink this same wine?" Logan scribbled some more on his note pad... "This is getting interesting." He looked at each of us. "And you have bottles of this brand of port wine in your coolers, yes? We would like to have a look at them...We will drop by your homes soon."

"I have a couple of bottles in my house and so does Jeb, I think. Both of us often bought this wine for Oli. We rib each other about it often... About this sweet-toothed family of ours. Must be in our genes..." Joseph attempted to smile as his voice trailed away.

"Well," Logan said. "The murder bottle, I mean the wine bottle, which had the poison, was almost empty and was on the rug. There was an unopened bottle of rum in the kitchen cabinet and an empty bottle of vodka in the recycling bin. We tested them. Both were clean."

Logan paused for a few minutes. "We think your sister must have laced the wine with the poison that Saturday evening. We couldn't find a container or bottle of this specific pesticide anywhere inside. She must have thrown it down the garbage chute. She then returned to the apartment and poured out the wine into tumblers... The garbage was cleared the next day and the container must already be in the Fleet Street landfill. It'll be tough to find.

"We will search for it anyway, although we don't know what we will be looking for...We found that a different kind of dangerous spray, chlorpyrifos insecticide, had been used around the beds and sofas in the apartment some time ago—maybe to get rid of bedbugs. That too is banned here...Couldn't find the container for that either."

He stared at us. "The strange things that people do, especially women. Wonder why she didn't leave a suicide note?... And wonder why she didn't think about her daughter?"

For another two hours, Logan wanted to know about our childhood, our parents, the schools we attended, the jobs we do, Olivia's life, her husband, her kids and our relationship with each other, even our close friends. He was probing, wanting to know little details. He didn't miss much and took a lot of notes. Jos and I drank several glasses of water.

Logan stood up at last. "We will transcribe the recording. You can leave now after signing the statements—they are all about what we spoke here in the room. We might call you for more information if needed, unless you want to add anything else."

Jos and I had nothing to tell each other on the way to the parking lot, although he kept saying, "Why did she...? Can't understand... Why did she..?

"What about Keira...?" I asked.

"Keira is fine for the moment. She is too young to grasp the situation. She watches TV most of the time; keeps her distracted and Jack and Joanne fuss over her."

I kept my head down, got into the car and drove away.

The bottle was not full when I gave it to Olivia. I drank a glass of the same port after dinner the previous Sunday... Where did the poison then come from? It has to be Gabriel, the bastard... Oh my God, oh no... it's the pesticide, that pesticide!

Reaching home, I bolted to the back of the house to the large shed in the backyard. Pushing aside the garden tools, a bag of lawn seeds, three bags of ice-melting salt and some paint cans, I went down on my knees and poked around in the corner. I couldn't find what I was looking for—a canister of pesticide that was left three years ago, along with boxes of assorted spray bottles and glass containers of disinfectants, by the previous owner of the house.

I remember the man, Darren, saying he ran a fumigation company in Caronport, some 60 km north of Regina. He said he would come back for it and I think we all forgot about it as time went by. That canister of phenol, I think it was—there was a label with proto-phosporous or potassium or something similar printed on it—must have been at least 30 years old, and had substances banned several years ago in Canada. It was right here in this corner...

Frantic now, I sprinted to the front of the house, opened the door and raced upstairs into my bedroom. Opening the mini wine cooler, I saw there were three full bottles of tawny port, and a half full bottle of red table wine on the shelves. Just as I had left it. God...

"Tsk-tsk," I heard a sucking sound behind me. I turned around and there was Audrey at the door, dressed in a tasteless black and white dress, showing off half her thighs and watching me. She had a hideous smile on her face.

"You think I don't know, you jerk? I knew it the day the police called you about Olivia. You poured that poison into the wine bottle you took over to Olivia on Saturday, didn't you? You think I wouldn't know?"

"What...What do you mean... I... I... I didn't... What garbage...?"

Her smile was gone as she hissed, "You bastard, that wine with the poison was meant to kill you. I mixed the fumigant in your shitty wine so that you will drink it and die and disappear from my life. Who knew you would go and kill your sister? You are such a scoundrel, you wouldn't give her a new bottle. You had to give her the opened one, right? Oh yes, you murdered them!"

I reeled back as if I was hit with a stun bolt gun and slumped on the edge of the bed. My stomach heaved as I retched. "What have you done? How could you... My God... Poor Olivia and Gabriel. Poor Keira." I punched the sides of my head with my fists.

Audrey was still lounging at the door, indifferent to my reaction. "I laced the bottle with the liquid from a canister lying in the shed. The label said it was a protoplasmic poison, and I wanted you to suffer severe diarrhoea, salivation and then poof..." She spat at me in an exaggerated action. "But you are so wretched, even death didn't want you."

I struggled to remain calm; and to fathom the enormity of the events unfolding over the past few days.

Think straight. If I mention the pesticide to Logan, I will be held culpable and be charged with murder or manslaughter.

"Did you think you could escape after killing me, Audrey?" I asked. "You would be the prime suspect."

Audrey was smug. Flipping her hair in that coquettish way when she wants to show disdain, she said, "Do you think I'm a fool? I planned it well, you idiot. I booked an audition in Toronto and was flying out on the morning of May 19, knowing that you will gulp down the entire bottle of this slop that evening; isn't every Sunday your drinking day? I prepared the shit for you—it was just Olivia's bad luck that she called you on the evening of the 18th, and you went and did this murder thing."

"But then you didn't go to Toronto on May 19..."

"I cancelled the audition and the tickets... After I knew what you had done... Just in case..."

"Just in case, what? I did not murder them," I shouted.

"Shhhh... Oh yes, you did. I now hold the aces, you creep." Audrey was triumphant. "You have always said that Gabs should be removed from this world, that Olivia is useless and that you wanted to adopt Keira. I can give that statement to the police."

"That was a long time ago... I was just talking out aloud."

"I am saving your skin, asshole. Tell the cops that you gave Olivia an unopened bottle. I have thrown away the canister of pesticide—just remember, it has your fingerprints."

"Threw away the container?... Where?"

"I dumped it somewhere along the Qu'Appelle River. Buried. Only I can get them... Or tell the police about it whenever the need arises. I will tell them you buried the stuff. By the way, do you know, I had also rehearsed the scene of your death. I would have found you in a pile of vomit and blood after I rushed back from Toronto, on hearing the news. I could have done a stellar act as a grieving widow in front of the police, your family and colleagues... I could have shown them my talent, beating my chest and crying, 'Oh, Jeb, my darling, what have you done?' And that you were despondent and suicidal because I wanted a divorce and was planning to relocate to Ontario. You spoiled the chance for my joyful histrionics, you scumbag, you freak!"

Wednesday, May 29. I was again at the office when Officer Logan called around noon. "We are wrapping up the case," he said. "Come to my office and I will brief you. I have spoken to your brother and he should also be here soon."

He led us to his office this time, not the interrogation room. After we sat down, Logan opened a folder and took out a sheet of paper. He scanned through it and said, "Dr. Anita Bergen, she's our forensic department head, suggests that both deaths were almost instantaneous. They had severe convulsions between 9:30 pm and 10:30 pm on Saturday, May 18.

"It could have been the carbon-nitrogen ions released by potassium cyanide soon after ingestion. We can't be sure yet because the poison dissipates soon. Olivia died about five or ten minutes after her husband died. Dr. Bergen has surmised that Olivia laced the wine with the pesticide, waited for Gabriel to drink his first glass and then consumed her potion. Their daughter must have slept by then."

Jos began weeping. I touched his shoulder, took a deep breath to try and keep calm. My heart seemed to swell up and fill my chest.

"We found Olivia worked in a pesticide warehouse as a temp about three months ago and she must have taken out a bottle of some fumigant that is banned in Canada. The warehouse inventory shows that someone listed three bottles, marked as hazardous, as missing for the past two years.... So her getting hold of it remains a puzzle... Maybe from some corner which had discarded items."

Logan was now reading from the file. "Note from secondary investigating officer: 'Olivia was a frequent visitor at the local food bank and always pleaded to be given extra food. Both Olivia's and Gabriel's bank accounts had very little money, and they owed a lot to a couple of loan companies. There was pressure and threats regarding payments.' I think this could have been the trigger for the atrocity."

He looked up and said, "We might investigate that angle later, but you see, our resources are stretched at the moment."

He pushed forward a couple of pages towards us. "These are application forms for you to fill up if you want us to release additional information and reports related to the case. The coroner is going to certify this incident as a murder-suicide and we will release the bodies to you in a couple of days. You can go ahead with the funeral arrangements. We will officially consider the case resolved and closed."

It was late evening when I reached home. On the way from the police station, Jos and I went to a downtown bar and had some drinks. We talked little, except to decide on a funeral home to arrange for the interments.

"You should have been here long ago," screamed Audrey as soon as I entered my home. Sitting in my living room, on my reclining sofa across from the TV, was a man in a grey suit, who got up and said he was Audrey's lawyer. He didn't shake my hand; just sat down again.

"I need my pound of flesh, Mr. Jacob Slater," Audrey intoned in theatrical style. "All the papers are ready for the divorce. You just have to sign them. We have to sell the house, of course, and you will have to give Mr. William Cantwell here statements about all your bank accounts, stocks, bonds and other holdings. He will verify them. Everything goes 50-50...We spoke about it the other day in you bedroom... By the wine cooler in your bedroom, didn't we?"

She sat on the arm of the sofa on which Cantwell was relaxing, as if it was his home, his legs stretched out. She cooed in his ears and ran her fingers through his hair. "We will settle things soon, won't we, Bill?"

"It should be a simple affair," said the shyster. "It's a straight, no-contest divorce; so there is no room for any acrimony. Mr. Slater will have no questions, I am sure; he can sign the papers and I will send a courier to pick them up in two days."

He got up and extended his hand to Audrey. "I think we should go, Audrey. Didn't you say you want to see the purple and gold interior decor and the ceiling mirrors in the bedroom of my penthouse condo?"

"Yes, of course. I am yearning to see your bawdy chambers, you delicious, sexy man," Audrey said. She turned towards me at the door. "So, until the day after, Jeb... You can even kiss me goodbye then." She laughed and struck a ballerina-like pose. "A proper kiss, with tongue, okay? And then you can get on with your life, with its shit-load of remorse."

You win, Audrey! Well played; I didn't see that move coming. I kept that pesticide all these years in the shed for the day when I could muster the courage to erase you from my life.

'Right' Side Of The Road

The fancy, branded woman's handbag in the trunk of my car was silken to the touch and had golden buckles and zippers. There was a 12-bottle case of premium vodka, alongside.

The time was 5:40 am. I was on Gloucester Street, east of the Rideau River, in front of the Bottingham Estates Condo complex in Ottawa. I had just dropped off two criminals who rode in my drive-share vehicle all the way from Pembroke—over 145 km.

One of them, Martino, a tall and distinguished looking man, who could pass off as a diplomat or a corporate lawyer, said, "Hey Watson, I have left your fare in a bag along with a gift in the trunk of your car."

He then waved to me and walked towards the building entrance, while his companion, a woman named Betty, blew a couple of kisses at me. I got back into the car with the bag and opened it. I counted five packets of new hundred-dollar bills; twenty to a packet; ten thousand dollars. My heart was now racing, my mouth dry.

Ten thousand dollars? What the fuck? Okay. And the case of vodka! A gift, a bribe, a bait?

I will now tell you the back story.

"Good evening, sir," I greeted the man, who exited the platform at the Oshawa GO station. He was wearing a stylish white suit; even his shoes were of white leather. His had striking features—reminiscent of a leading man in a classic Western film. It was around 7:30

pm, already nighttime on a mid-November weekend. It was cold and there was a hint of fog.

"Evening, guy," he said, as he got into the back seat and I hefted his hard shell suitcase into the trunk of the car.

I switched on the engine, drove out onto the road and was nearing the exit to the 401 towards Morningside when the passenger, Monty Berten, leaned forward and tapped me on my right shoulder.

"Stop, Watson. That is your name, right? Can you please turn off the GPS, change direction and take me to the outskirts of Pembroke."

I shook my head and said, "Sir, the ride is booked for Morningside. I cannot change the route. Pembroke is in the other direction and too far away for me. It's over four hours of driving and it will be midnight when we reach there... And I have to be home."

Every weekend, I get passengers who want this, that or the other, most of them drunks or prostitutes whom I pick up outside bars late in the night in my ride share taxi. Some of them demand that I bring them water or soft drinks and chips from convenience stores; some want sandwiches from drive-through restaurants. Some are so addled on drugs that they forget their belongings in the car, and I have to hunt for them the next day or hand them over at the police station. There have been a couple of times when passengers have threatened violence and robbed me of all my cash. Of course, there are some passengers who are well-mannered and give a good tip.

I am a meek sort of person and my friends always exhort me to be more assertive with people. I can't. I am just made like that. My daughter chides me by saying, 'Your spirit animal is a sheep, daddy.' And I reply, "Yes, girl. I am like a timid and docile sheep."

I heard a loud click and there was Mr. Berten, now holding a curved, serrated knife, with holes like Swiss cheese, in front of my face. "Switch off the rideshare GPS and drive me to Pembroke. Here, you can use my phone for directions. I have already entered the address. Now, if you want to live..." He handed me his phone.

"Yes...yes...sir, sir," I stammered. My mouth was parched.

Flicking the knife close, he settled back in his seat and said in a buttery voice, "Don't press that alarm button. I won't hurt you, Watson. Just take me there. Don't take the highway. Use the side roads. It's all there in my GPS."

"It's going to be foggy tonight, sir. I don't know the route. Can we take the highway for some distance, at least? It is safer."

"Let's stick to the back roads... And I also have a gun, okay? A shot can shatter your spine."

I hate the side roads at night. There are no street lights, sparse traffic, few homes, expansive fields, and woods with trees on either side, ghostly and menacing at this time of the year, and the thought of a deer leaping in front of my car terrifies me.

His GPS showed me his destination as Brumsfield in the Laurentian Valley, Renfrew County. Terrified, I turned around, headed to King Street, took Taunton Road, steered left on Concession Road that merged with Jewel Road, took a right on Ganaraska Road and then on to Northumberland Country Rd. 28—a long, long drive.

My God, I have never heard of these roads and how do I reach this bloody Brumsfield, while driving in the dark? Who is this guy I have picked up? How can I connect with the police? He will slice my throat... Or shoot me.

"C'mon, Watson, you can drive faster. There won't be any cops on these roads." He laughed. "You have a funny name... Watson!"

"It's Valsan, sir, not Watson."

"I like to call you Watson. Heard of him? He was a brilliant detective, sidekick of Sherlock Holmes"

"Yes, but they were not real people..."

"So Watson, don't try any shamus tricks with me, okay?"

"What's shamus, sir?"

"Oh, nothing, just a joke. Where are you from, Watson? Trinidad, Guyana, Fiji or Sri Lanka?"

"No sir, I am from India. From Kerala, it's a southern province. I am a mechanical engineer, just driving in the evenings to make some extra cash." I wanted to keep talking to soothe my nerves. "Can't get good jobs, so I have been working part time in an auto body shop in the mornings for the past five years..."

"Usual sob story...What do you make from the auto shop?"

"About $18,000 a year."

"That's real shit money, man. Why do you guys come here and work in these jobs?

"Our kids will do well here, sir. That is our hope. That is why we all come here."

"I am from Barbados... And St. Lucia and Jamaica and Louisiana —I roam around the entire Caribbean and the United States. It's my kingdom, you see. I also lived in England and Italy for many years, Watson. You know the West Indies?"

"Yes, sir. For their cricket."

"Ha ha, yes. You have two children, right, Watson?"

"Two sir... daughter and son, both in school. How did you...?

"And your wife works in a supermarket. And you just make enough to pay the rent and for food, right?"

"Yes sir. But, how did you...Why?"

"I know all about you... Just testing you to see if you are telling the truth... I know you are from India. I also know that you hold a technology patent for reinforcing the steering wheel casings of many types of vehicles. And there is another one pending about brake fluid mechanics, right? You should be doing well in Canada, you know, with your knowledge. Sad, Watson, sad."

I was now driving through the woods of Bowmanville. There was some light from lamp posts at intersections that loomed at intervals, but the darkness was getting worse. I switched on the high-beam lights and saw the trees flashing by. The rear windshield appeared as if someone had tarred it black. Dense, murky fog closed the road and the woods behind us.

Inside, I could see the blue light from Berten's GPS phone on my dashboard and the radiance from a phone that he was fiddling with behind me. His voice pierced through the purr of the car engine. "I have your address here, man. Valsan Thomas of 203, 144 Dagwood

Avenue, Oshawa. Aha... a small rental apartment."

He was now speaking on the phone. "Hey Dingo, take Amos with you and go to that address. Yes, the same. I am texting some instructions to you, okay? You know what to do... Tell Baron where you are going. I will call you when I reach Brumsfield."

He was quiet for about five minutes, typing something. His phone rang. "Yes, Dingo. That's right. 144 Dagwood. Read my text. man. Yes, yes, it's the same driver you told me about...Top of the list."

"Hey Watson, my men will be at your apartment building in 20 minutes. For your protection. Now you behave fine, okay?"

I was breathing deep, trying to stop the panic attack that I could see coming. My stomach churned. "What is happening, sir? Whom did you give my address to? Why? I am taking you to Brumsfield. There is no problem, sir. I mean...What is this top of the list?"

"Don't turn your head, man. Look straight ahead. I told you, it's for their protection, your protection, our protection. Don't worry. Just drive. Oh, the list... Just names of some of the best drivers and mechanics in Oshawa."

"Why...Why didn't you ask one of your men to drive you to Brumsfield, sir?"

"Many people know about our cars and our guys. Undesirables, like nosy and unfriendly police officers, some social justice thugs." He was laughing now. "And some of the underworld types, you see. But you are the best, Watson. You are a nobody, yet. I think we can always depend on people like you. I cancelled two rides before you picked up the order."

In the patchy fog, which was now thinning out, I saw a skunk slink across the road. I braked hard; the creature stood transfixed for a moment in the headlights, then ambled away.

"Are you thinking of ways to get rid of me, or what?" Berten chuckled. 'You trying to crash the car?"

This is so intolerable. It's my car. Let me see what he does. I must not allow him to push me. I mean, there is a limit to this... I may be a docile sheep, but there is some steel within me.

Pulling the car to the side of the road, I switched off the engine and said, "I must call my wife and tell her I will be late."

Berten took out a gun from a holster under his coat and pointed it at my head. "Did I tell you to stop the car? I have no problem with shooting you. I will count to three and we better get going. One..."

"Okay...okay, but let me call home."

He put the gun back. "Just a second." He spoke into his phone. "Hey Amos, you there? Fine, his wife and kids are home? Okay, keep the watch. Send me a picture, pronto, *velocemente*."

A few minutes later, he showed me a shot of my apartment building, and pictures showing my wife arriving after her shift, lights in our living room on the second floor, and in one of the bed rooms.

"See, I told you they are all fine. You can call your wife and tell her you have a long-distance fare to Ottawa and will be late. Nothing else, okay? Amos, who is parked on your street, is a bit of a weirdo, and has a sharp temper. So..."

I called my wife. "Hey Jessie, don't worry. I have got a long trip and will be late...Will be home after midnight, hopefully. Are the kids asleep? And don't wait up for me. Yes, yes, a single passenger, going to Ottawa. Fine. See you soon."

We are now deep in rural north Ontario. There are large farms with farmhouses, spaced far apart. The fog had descended and covered the entire area like a white, silken veil. Faint lights twinkled far away at intervals. There were signs on the road saying 'Wildlife Crossing'. I switched on the fog lights. I prayed.

Oh, God, let there not be any deer leaping across the road... Let there be no moose or elk or wolves. No there won't be wolves. But these roads border the Algonquin Park, which has wolves. Don't let the car break down. Berten, you bastard. You will die a thousand deaths. You will rot in hell!

We drove through Third Line and branched into Heritage Line, which was also County Road 34. I kept the speed at a steady 50 kph, sometimes slowing to 40 kph. Berten grumbled, saying I was driving too slow on an empty road.

"There are ditches on either side of the road and wire fences beyond, and I don't want us to crash," I said. "I can't drive much faster in this fog."

Some farms still had rows of corn standing on either side, phantom figures waiting to swallow motorists making a wrong turn in the night's murkiness.

In the rearview mirror, I saw Berten take out a bottle from his hand luggage, open the cap and take several huge gulps. "Do you want a drink of vodka, Watson? Do you ever drink?"

"No, never while driving and yes, I drink vodka or scotch on the weekends. And never straight from the bottle. That is uncouth."

"That's good... You got me there... I like my crystal ware too. Hey, with a surname like Thomas, looks like you come from a religious family, right? Do you pray?" He chuckled. "I am a spiritual person. I follow any spirit that is dominant at a given time."

My mood was as dark as the night outside. "No, I am not very religious, but there should be some moral standards to follow."

"Morals? If you feel good when you do something, then it's moral. You should answer only to yourself. Got it, Watson?"

This is deer and moose country. The terror of hitting one of them bolting across the road kept my eyes peeled. We were on the ON-28 north—a drive of about two hours at a stretch before we hit Renfrew County. I cursed myself for picking up this passenger. So desolate was the entire region that only a single car had traveled in the opposite direction so far.

Two and a half hours out of Oshawa, I told Berten, "I will need gas. I just saw a sign about a 24-hour general store and gas station on Wolverine Road about 5 km ahead. Can we stop there?"

"Yeah, of course. I need a coffee too," Berten said. "And stretch my legs. You are a skillful driver, Watson. Yes, an excellent driver; and a damn talented engineer, I know."

While I filled the gas, Berten walked into the store. There was only one car on the lot and when I went in, he had ordered a dozen doughnuts, two chicken sandwiches and two large coffees. He paid for all of it in cash. "Mustn't leave any trail, Watson," he whispered into my ear. "The doughnuts are for my boys on the farm."

There were no customers in the dining area. The car in the lot must belong to the lone employee at the counter. We ate the warmed-up sandwiches in silence and drank our coffees.

Berten stared at me. "You had a criminal case for murder in your hometown of Panoor, didn't you? You allowed a hoist holding up a vehicle to fall on one of your co-workers, didn't you?"

"What, how did you?... How...? That was an accident... One of the levers was faulty. The case was withdrawn and I was discharged."

"But you had an ongoing quarrel with that man—and there's another assault case and an attempt-to-murder charge in your local police file. You didn't mention those in your immigration papers... Don't worry... Your secrets are safe with me, okay?" Berten smiled.

We went back to the car. Tired, and with a heavy migraine because of the intense focus on the steering wheel, I turned the car at last into Renfrew Road, and took Foymount Road and then onto Hwy 41 in Eganville. It's a highway of the old kind, not the four-lane or six-lane kind in the GTA. Open farmlands rushed behind us.

How the hell did he get that information from police in my native place? What connections does this bastard have? Hope my family is safe—with Berten's goons outside our home. Who are these guys?

The Eganville drive was a hellish one—a full hour of misery, with Berten dozing off much of the time. I thought of stopping somewhere to, drag the bastard out and throw him into a ditch and go home. But then what? What about Amos and Baron and Dingo and other gangsters this guy has under his control? They have my address, so a police complaint is also ruled out.

We were now passing through roads like Heritage Lane, Drummond Line and Base Line. We hit MacKay Street and the Pembroke region at last.. .The GPS said 35 minutes to Brumsfield.

Berten was now awake and taking another swig from the bottle. "How are you, Watson?" The buttery voice had returned. "I will give you a good tip over the taxi fare, okay?"

"I don't want any tip, sir. I just want to go home."

He was now on the phone, speaking in a mixture of some broken English and French. *Kenbe salo sa yo mare. Mwen pral fè fas ak yo pita.* (Keep those bastards tied up. I will deal with them later.) I heard strange names like Bibby, Lupo, Beanie and Martino.

"Don't look so puzzled, Watson. It's Haitian Creole. You won't understand. I speak many languages. If you take me to your home, I can learn your language in two months. And stop looking at me. Focus on the road...We will be there soon."

We reached the town of Brumsfield and Berten was suddenly alert. His face was near my ear as he ordered, "Go right past Main Street and then make a left turn at the next intersection. Just drive easy."

Some 15 minutes after the turn, we reached an unpaved side road that led to an open wooden gate, which had a barbed wire fence running on both sides for a considerable distance. A menacing signboard proclaimed it as 'Bucklebelt Farms - Private Property', along with a dim spotlight on a skull and bones image. I stopped the car and Berten said, "Go straight on. Your car springs should be fine."

We bumped along a winding track of mud and small rocks, with woods on either side, for another 10 minutes, and reached a well-lit clearing, fenced with mesh wire. On one side of an imposing. ranch-style farm-house was a huge barn. Three tractor-trailers and some rail containers with windows and doors were parked in front, along with several black SUVs, ATVs and motorcycles.

"We are here," said Berten, as he got out of the car, stretching his arms and shaking his legs.

Several people appeared out of nowhere—white men, black men and brown men and two white women. They waited their turn to shake hands and hug Berten; three of the men thumped me on my back and said "Hi Watson." One of them lifted the luggage from the trunk and took it into a container.

"See, they know all about you," Berten was all smiles. "You can call your wife if you want and tell her that you will be home late in the morning. You can make up an excuse. I know you will."

There was country music coming from inside the ranch house,

along with the smoky smell of roasting beef or chicken. A couple of fire pits in the clearing crackled and blazed, and kept the cold away.

Berten's demeanor, however, changed in an instant. Gone was the affableness as he took off his jacket and handed it to one of the men. "Where are they, Lupo? Did they talk?"

"In the barn, Monty...Waiting for you."

"Let's go." He pulled out his gun from his shoulder holster and walked towards the huge barn that towered like an ogre in the shadows. The others followed him, and one of them took the car fob and key from me. "Stay where you are. Don't move and don't get into the car for now."

The time was around 2:00 in the morning. I reached into the car to take out a bottle of water and my cellphone. "Hey Jessie," I told my wife, after she picked up the phone on the first ring. "I am fine. I am in Ottawa. There was some problem and a detour on the 401; so we were late getting here."

"You don't sound right," she said.

"No, no, I am fine, just a little tired and now sitting in a coffee shop. There's a lot of fog here. I will wait for it to clear a little and then start for home. Don't worry, I will be there by the morning. Are the kids...?"

Two muffled shots rang out from the barn, shattering the inertia of the night. "I will call later..."

My heart thumped, and I cowered behind the car. Two more loud plops followed like rapid echoes. I poked my head over the car trunk, and five minutes later saw Berten come out of the barn, unscrewing a long cylinder from his gun, as he walked towards the ranch house. A few minutes later, others emerged from the barn; four of the men dragged two bodies by their legs across the gravel.

In the grotesque and shape-shifting shadows of the clearing, I saw the victims had their hands behind them and their chests were bloody. The head on one body was half blown away. The coppery smell of blood raked my nostrils as I huddled in terror, holding on to the rim of a front tire of my car.

This is murder. Oh my God, I am a witness to two murders. I will also be implicated in this. What do I do now? These hoodlums will kill me, too. Why did I ever become a taxi driver?

I crept out from behind the car and stood there, trembling. "Don't kill me, please. I haven't seen anything. I won't tell anybody. Please...Please."

"These guys were killers. They have destroyed many lives in New Orleans. We can't let them go free, can we? God wouldn't like it, right?" Berten was waving his gun around and talking to no one in particular. "These guys didn't want to talk, didn't want to listen. That's not good, right? So we had to make them go kaput." He turned towards me. "And Watson, you are right. You haven't seen anything... Or heard anything. Remember that."

"You are a good judge, Monty," one man yelled.

"Can I go home now? Please, Mr. Berten?"

"In an hour or so, Watson. I need to talk to you first...You want to be with your wife and kids, don't you?"

The men went to work with machine-like efficiency. They stripped the bodies of their clothes, belts and shoes and gathered them in an oil drum, emptied a two-gallon jerry can full of gasoline and set them on fire.

Aghast and choked up, I watched them wrap the bodies in mats and tie them up with ropes. One of the women, a slim, almost flat-chested woman—they called her Betty—was taking the most active part in the work. She seemed to be enjoying herself, smirking at me often. The other woman stood watching.

Berten gesticulated and harangued the group '*fè travay la anvan maten*' (Get the job done before morning); '*Vini non, vini, netwaye vit*' (Come on, come on, quick.)

He shouted out again, walking up and down. "Hey Watson, help them take away these pieces of shit. Lupo, you ride with Watson and we'll meet you at the Bonnecherra end of the farm."

Two of the men carried a body to a vehicle, which now had its engine running and the rear door open. They threw the body in, its limbs askew and hitting the door frame. I shuddered.

"Hold the legs of this guy," one of the men ordered me. "We are going to put him in your car." Another man grabbed the head, and we lifted the body. I was nauseous. I have never touched a naked male body before, although it was now covered in sack cloth. It felt light for such a big-boned human being.

"Come on, drive," Lupo prodded me. Both of us got into the car. It was a huge farm. We drove for about 15 minutes on soft mud tracks with cabbage and kale planted on either side. After a few twists and turns, we reached another enormous barn at one end of the farm. Behind it were thick woods, inky dark even without any foliage on the trees. Clumps of dry bushes ran along the tree line.

"Don't think a lot about what you saw at the farmhouse," Lupo said. "Those guys were both on the FBI's most wanted list and one of them was also in the cross-hairs of Canada's CSIS. Nobody will miss them. They are better off dead."

I drove into the barn. The other SUV was already there, and the men were dragging out the body, near what looked like a huge industrial garbage bin on steel legs, with a box-like structure on the side, with switches and levers.

"We burn things here. Critters, dried plants and things that make organic ash fertilizer for our vegetable plants. So no contaminants like shoes and clothes," said Lupo, with a snicker. "Come on, let's dump this creature."

Both bodies were heaved into the bin. One of the women went to the switchboard, turned a couple of dials and pulled down a lever. An engine whirred, the bin vibrated and settled into a steady hum. My stomach churned, and I threw up. I leaned against a beam and Lupo handed me a bottle of water.

"This will take about three hours," Berten said. "Hey Bibbi, you stay here until the morning. Come on guys and you, Watson, let's go to the house."

Everyone removed their shoes before entering. The interior had lavish decor. There was a long bar at one end of the huge living room area and Berten and his band sat on high stools. Martino lifted a couple of bottles of vodka from the bar rails and began pouring into glasses. Recessed lighting created warm shadows, and a diffused glow in the room. Bright rugs in brilliant patterns covered much of the floor, and large tapestries hung on the walls. Assorted plants and ferns covered an entire wall of the room. Winter and violence seemed like a far-away dream. This looked a like a cozy party of friends.

For over an hour, I heard their banter and laughter and asinine jokes. Piled high on plates before us were strips of tender beef and assorted varieties of chicken wings, along with shot glasses for many spirits. The aroma of jerk chicken and the roast beef was tantalizing, and I ate like a glutton. I didn't leave the rum-glazed ice-cream and the strawberry cheesecake either.

Berten took me to a corner, where he settled down in a leather reclining chair and signalled for me to sit beside him on an ottoman. He spoke softly about life and death. "Destiny is what we choose when there are questions before us," he said. "Destiny is the plunge we take." He spoke about how we must seize opportunities, how we can shape our future and decide on the happiness quotient for our families. "Poverty cannot create poetry or make you inventive."

On the walls, there were several large photographs of Berten with several Canadian political and business leaders. "Oh, that one, you know him. He is one vociferous MP; the picture was taken last year when we were sailing in the waters off the Bahamas."

He pointed at another gilt-framed picture. "This guy on the golf range, you know him, he is from the opposition benches pictured in the Dominican Republic on a sponsored visit. And this politician in the blue suit who wants a harsher crackdown on crime—we were in Las Vegas. Everybody is sold out, Watson. Everybody, everywhere, charts their own roads."

They have such an eventful life. I envy them. No shortage of money, enjoying the good things. Look at the plush decor... Why is my life so harsh, such a continuous struggle? Why should I be bullied by the thuggish manager at the auto shop? My life is mundane, exhausting, with nothing to hope for... Nothing for the children's future... This is the life I want... This is the life I want for my family.

"Here, Watson, take a couple of shots,' Martino called out. "This will calm your stomach."

"No, I can't. I can't drive after I drink. My head starts buzzing."

"Oh, you will, you will... One day, we are going to take you to the Caribbean and immerse you in a rum-filled tub in our resorts in Aruba or Jamaica or wherever. Cheers to that!"

Berten finally stood up. The time was 4:00 am. "You can go now, Watson. Drop Betty and Martino off on Gloucester Street in Ottawa, and then head home on the 401 to be with your family."

"Are they going to kill me on the way?" Once again, I found myself quivering with fear.

Berten guffawed. "You are a funny man, Watson. We could have killed you so many times by now. You are our man, I told you. We look after our people. You are a great driver, a top mechanic, and we will need you again."

He moved a finger across his lips. "Your lips are zipped, Watson, and... And we know all about your family. Now scram. Do what you have to do. Live your life and revel in its big and little pleasures."

Betty chimed in, "Have you seen the Judge Dredd movies, Watson? Monty is our top judge. He judges and carries out sentences. He is a true judge of character, and he has judged you."

"Our Monty is also a lawyer, accredited in two provinces here in Canada, Louisiana in the United States and he has great connections in the Caribbean," Martino said.

One hour and 45 minutes later, we arrived in Ottawa, in front of the Bottingham Estates. And it was here that I opened the car trunk and found the handbag with cash and the case of vodka. It was a dilemma, all right. A problem for which I could think of no solution. What do I do with the money? How could I go to the police without endangering the life of my family? What do I tell my wife? Should I just throw away this blood money, burn it or dump it in a church collection box?

As mentioned before, I am a submissive person, and believe that God wills everything. He opens the doors; He shows us the way; He guides us. So I chose to keep the money. I decided to tell my wife that I got a thousand dollars from the Ottawa trip and tell her more lies about long-distance fares in the coming days or about overtime work at the auto shop to account for the bonanza.

It was around 11:00 am when I reached home. Fortunately, the Sunday traffic was light and two brief halts at OnRoute rest station coffee shops kept me alert on the 401.

My children greeted me with excitement; my wife was pacing the room. She paused and said, "You look terrible, go take a shower and freshen up. You need to sleep."

In the bathroom mirror, a dishevelled, haggard and exhausted face looked back at me.

What a hellish day. Keep calm, don't look so drained. Smile. Tell them it was a good day. It was a good day. Yes, it was a good day!

After a quick shower and shave, I came into the drab living room and found my wife and children, bright-eyed and animated, sitting on sofas we bought at a flea market. I looked around. The fittings in the room were old and shabby, the curtains scruffy, the linoleum on the floor cracked up and streaky.

A soft, leather briefcase was on the coffee table. "Here's a present for you, Valsan Thomas Daddy, from a Mister Somebody for his honesty. Let's give him a round of applause," my daughter Jenny announced as if she was addressing a big audience on her school annual day.

"Two men came here at around 8 o'clock this morning. Both were tall and stylishly dressed," my wife said, her hand on the briefcase. "They said you returned a suitcase containing over half million dollars in bonds and cash cheques to the Flagginton Credit Union office last month. One of their managers had forgotten it in your car. You didn't tell me about it... Like other times when you return lost and found things."

"Oh yes, oh yes, I remember," I lied. "A month ago. I thought it was just a suitcase full of clothes. Didn't think it was very important. I find so many things in the car... Even dentures and tampons."

"Well, one man was thin and bald and his name was Amos Simon. The other man, I didn't get his name, it was something like Ringo or Jingo—he had a big belly. Both said they were officers at the bank. This man Amos said this briefcase was a gift for returning the money, but they didn't want any publicity because it would affect their image—if it was known that a bank manager had misplaced so much of cash."

My son Vincent jumped up and said, "They also gave us these two iPads," holding aloft the iconic devices.

"They came in, they sat here, ate some cookies and drank tea before they left," my wife said. "Very cultured people—they were here for about an hour. That Amos was always quoting from the Bible." She turned to the children. "Okay, you two, go to your rooms and take the iPads with you."

I was getting impatient. "Did they say anything else, I mean...? What's in the briefcase?"

"Open it. I already did—didn't want the children to see it."

Stacks of hundred-dollar bills were packed to fill almost three-quarters of the briefcase, and covered in bubble wrap. My eyes bulged.

"Twenty thousand dollars," my wife said in a hushed voice. "That is a big gift. It's true that when you do good and honest things, God will open the windows of heaven to shower blessings on his children. Thank you, God, oh, thank you!"

Berten was pulling me deeper into his web. I had nothing to say to my wife.

Two weeks later, a manager from the Oshawa office of Flagginton called me. Flora O'Brien introduced herself and said, "Mr. Thomas, we have approved your application for a business loan of $800,000 to purchase the Lugs and Plugs Auto Shop in North Oshawa."

Stunned, because that was the place I go to work every day, I said, "Ms O'Brien, I have not applied for any loan from your bank... And... Who...?"

She cut me off. "Oh yes, we have all the proper documents, including valuation of all your assets and a guarantor for the special, low-interest loan—Montgomery Berten of Ottawa. There is also the purchase agreement for the auto shop along with all its equipment. All we need is for you to come in anytime this week, open an account with us and sign off on some of these papers."

O'Brien's voice dropped a notch. "Mr. Berten is one of the directors on the bank board and he is a very persuasive man. It's difficult to say no to him. He has also underlined something in a note here... It reads, 'I know Mr. Valsan Thomas very well and he knows me. He is like a brother to me.'"

Brother? Why did he do that? Does he want me to service their murder vehicles or contraband cars in the auto shop? I have already taken their money. What other crimes will they pull me into? What do I do now? What to do? What to do?

As you know by now, I am not a fighter, so I succumbed again. Early next morning, I went to the bank, where the staff greeted me like a millionaire customer and I signed all the documents. A week later, I took charge of the Lugs and Plugs Auto Shop, recruited a new batch of well-recommended technicians, whose appointments I couldn't reject. My set of beliefs had changed, because my world itself had lost its moral direction. Keeping the system running was now of paramount importance... And business boomed.

My wife and I had promised during our early days of courtship never to have any secrets between us. However, I have never mentioned Monty Berten or our trip to Pembroke... And I never will.

Four eventful years have gone by, and so did my niggling money problems. There are always expensive cars being brought in for service in the auto shop, many of which are then sent by truck to Montreal. Ordinary cars come to have their engines souped up and SUVs drive in to get special compartments built under the chassis and under the floorboards. This is, of course, done in a sealed off section of the shop. Cash, well above the amount on the invoices, pours in and I have to expand to keep up with the demand.

Today, I am the primary owner of seven Lugs and Plugs workshops across the GTA and more will open next year. Everything is legitimate; a legal department gives advice on every company move. My family is very happy with the realization of our Canadian Dream. I am working on a new invention, related to magnets and energy density in EV engines.

"Shouldn't we move into our own nice home, instead of this slum-like apartment?" I asked my family over three years ago.

You can imagine the response. We bought a large estate home in the upscale Taunton area of Oshawa. My wife is today the vice-president of the Oshawa Horticultural Society and also a member of the fund-raising committee for the Durham Hospital Network. My children will be in university in a couple of years. They say they want to go and study in England. So be it!

I don't drive a ride-share car anymore, but own a full-service taxi company, with a fleet of ten cars which are rented out to drivers for a daily fee. Lupo, Beanie, Amos, Martino and many others are my close acquaintances. Martino is also on the Lugs and Plugs management board. They help out whenever I call them to deal with an unpleasant outsider in the shop or other government-type people whom I cannot mention here. They are boisterous guests at my garden barbecues, along with their wives and girlfriends. Local political bigwigs, city managers from Oshawa and neighbouring towns and some councillors are also occasional guests at my home.

Remember Betty, the flat-chested woman at Brusmsfield? She is a senior police officer in Louisiana. When I was in that state a couple of months ago, she showed me around her beautiful city on the Mississippi River, took me out to dinner and invited me home to meet her husband and children. She also suggested that it was time for me to run for a city council seat in Oshawa.

As for Monty Berten, I still don't know who he is or what he does and if he has killed many people. I have never spoken about him to any of our 'team' members. He comes to the Oshawa GO station once in every three months or so and calls for Watson. I pick him up in one of the standard cabs and drop him off at his mansion in the Kawartha Lakes area, or at a lake-facing penthouse condo in downtown Toronto, or his cottage in Muskoka. He has, however, never asked me to take him to Brumsfield again, and has declined all invitations to visit my home. "Later, Watson... Maybe one day."

Still, I put on a dramatic shudder every time he gets into my car, not the back seat, but the front passenger seat. At the start of our long, pleasant, night-time drives, he taps my shoulder and whispers, "Hey Watson, I have a gun, okay?" He then laughs aloud.

"Yes, Judge," I reply. "I too have a gun! I also have a curved, serrated knife, that has holes like Swiss cheese. You gave me those, remember? I hope never to use them!"

"I heard you have already beaten up some people. I have been told that you have to be pulled away when you get violent. Fond of boxing, eh? Control... Control is essential, Watson!"

"Only minor assaults, Judge. Happens sometimes, but weapons, no—not so far. I am trying to manage my temper."

During the drive, Monty talks of politics and economics in Latin America and the Caribbean islands and what ought to be done to create egalitarian societies in those countries. His words are like the drip-drip of water that wears down and shapes a rock, like breaking waves that rearranges shorelines, like a pollinator—seeding our brains with ideas that can be soaked up with ease.

For me, it feels good to be a bright planet in an exuberant orbit around Monty—for now. I always remind myself that my spirit animal is still the sheep, but with some twisted DNA of the wolf. So, I will bide my time. As learned men have always said, the road that the righteous travel is bright and scenic, even in the darkest of the nights. Who is to judge, anyway...?

Psst... You Will Listen To Me!

Armed with a large, sharp knife, I will stand in front of my full-length washroom mirror, whisper a few words, and slash my stomach from left to right. I will watch my intestines tumble out. Yes, *hara-kiri/seppuku* will be the ritualistic way to end it all... to avoid capture, or perhaps to atone for my many sins.

I am fascinated by the honourable way the Samurai of Japan chose to end their lives, after major mission failures. I will do the same when the world closes in on me, and when I feel I can do no more.

The young woman, around 28 years old, stood still on the sidewalk of a main road in North York and lifted her baby from its stroller beside her.

She was wearing a bright red and yellow frock with a little straw hat on her head and was about 10 or 15 feet away from the bus stop. Appearing a little irritable and disoriented, she looked all around her, as if yearning for some prompt or some signal. Three other people were busy on their phones in the shelter, waiting for the southbound bus. The mid-July sun was scorching, as expected, around 4:00 pm. Traffic was heavy on the road.

Assuming the set position of a baseball pitcher, the young woman hurled the baby in front of the approaching bus. The driver braked hard and the heavy, articulated vehicle hit a van in the other lane. It swerved to the right again and veered onto the curb. Several cars ended in a pile-up as they rear-ended the ones in front. Amidst the screeching and clanging of metal, people screamed as blood spilled beneath the rear wheels of the bus.

The mob acted in predictable fashion, with some people rushing towards the site of the crash and others fleeing from it. It was just like I imagined, a movie being projected in front of me. This is an edge-of-the-seat thriller; the ultimate in gory entertainment. More people were coming out from the small shops on either side, like ghouls gathering for a morbid feast.

The rasping sound of a fire truck horn and the piercing sirens of police and other emergency vehicles grew louder as they approached. The woman stood motionless at the crash site, arms raised high and howling, 'Ahhhhhhh.'

I had seen the woman just 30 minutes earlier at the coffee shop in the strip mall on the corner of Jane Street and Bathurst Street. Sitting at a table nearby, she was eating a strawberry strudel and cooing to a baby in a stroller by her chair. Everything was well with her world. Outside, it was sunny, with beautiful people going about their day-to-day businesses. She glanced at me once. That was enough.

While sipping from my large cup of flavored coffee, I whispered to her, "Death is the release when all glory will be revealed."

"Life is not meant to be enjoyed. Life is intended for penance and hardship. We must suffer life, not live it. Suffering is a virtue and we ought to rejoice in it, so get rid of your baby," I whispered again. "Throw the tot under a bus." The words wafted away and were imprinted in her mind, as I knew it would.

She looked at me again, this time with glazed eyes, blinked once, rubbed her eyes and walked out with the stroller. She left her half-eaten strudel and her untouched iced drink on the table.

I don't like this concept of happiness for no reason. The average human being is an idiot who is always trying to conform to attitudes and behaviours of people around him or her—to become 'normal'. You might not agree with me, but my thoughts are better than your ideas and my ways are always right. And this is what I believe...

The woman was still howling and beating her chest as two policewomen restrained her. The crowd was milling around the bus and the wrecked cars as other police officers tried to push them towards the pedestrian walkway.

I smiled as I walked away from the scene. The young woman had played her part just as I directed her. By next week, a panel of psychiatrists will conclude that she was suffering from deep postpartum depression and place her in an institution. They will say she was also full of self-destructive urges, especially after learning that her husband was having an affair with one of her close friends.

'Daniela Rojas is not criminally responsible for the violent act of killing her baby. She has repeatedly said, after extensive psychoanalysis, that she heard a voice in her head, commanding her to kill,' the doctors will write in their report.

Poor Daniela, she will have to spend a minimum of three years being monitored round-the-clock in a cell, and heavily medicated, before she can be considered for release into a safe house.

Waves of euphoria washed over me. This third launch has been an eye-catching and mind-bending accomplishment.

Let me tell you about the other two launches.

A busy Monday morning. I am standing near the escalator of Wellesley station on the Yonge–University Line 1. Both platforms are packed with commuters. Leaning against a pillar, I am scanning the faces of people rushing by, much like the intrusive facial recognition systems now being employed by security forces everywhere.

What I see in front of me is a mother lode of gold. For prospectors like me, there are nuggets and ingots aplenty—people with deep emotional fault lines, people living without hope of any financial betterment, widows, widowers, unhappy immigrants, diseased individuals, scumbags, criminals, and other riff-raff living on the margins of society... The list is rich with possibilities. The little antennae—in every strand of hair at the front of my head—can identify such worthless creatures.

I settled on a young South Asian man, looking up an at information board, lit up in green, He was well-dressed, in a navy blue suit, with a trendy, crew hair cut and I surmised he could be a new immigrant—a computer professional—going to attend an interview at one of the big banks or insurance firms downtown.

"Alas, your day will not end well, young man," my whisper floated over the heads of the throng and into the ears of my victim. He must have got my message. He looked around him and our eyes met for a second. He wiggled a finger in his right ear. Bingo!

"Do you see that woman with grey hair, wearing a blouse with pink flowers and matching skirt, a leather handbag slung across her shoulder?" I murmured. "Look, she is touching her hair and now moving towards the yellow marker line on the platform. Go rush her, young man. Push her onto the tracks just as the train enters the station. Go...," I hissed.

Scores of people screamed a minute later. The noise was like a drum roll that rose and rumbled across the station as the train screeched to a halt. The woman with the grey hair was gone... Some commuters were tackling, racking and mauling the bewildered young man and piling upon him. There were others using their cellphones to capture the commotion for their social media posts. It was chaos, just as I imagined. The launch of my first individual contact program was a masterful display of mind power.

Media reports the next day explained it as:

"A young immigrant pushed an elderly woman onto the tracks, in front of an oncoming train at the Wellesley station The identities of the victim and the perpetrator are not being disclosed, until preliminary investigations are completed.

Police said the victim and the assailant are not known to each other. The assailant was not known to the police. Train services were disrupted for over four hours on the Yonge–University Line 1 and passengers were asked to take special TTC shuttle buses to the next station."

Mental imbalance, what else? Canadians are great proponents of mental illness theories. Depression, suicidal thoughts and unheard of behavioural syndromes afflict over half our population. Such beings are ideal prey for geniuses like me.

The young man will spend several years in psychiatric wards—or mental hospitals, as they were called earlier—before being released into the custody of his parents or deported if he had not yet acquired

Canadian citizenship. Oh, his poor folk!

The relatives of the elderly woman would be overjoyed. Gone, cut under the wheels of a train. There could be a substantial insurance payout. She will soon be forgotten. Who wants to remember useless and bloated old fogies? Anyway, it's not my job to theorize on morals or justify things I do to enhance my brainpower.

I realized that I had the talent to control weaker minds at a very early age—at around the age of four, to be precise. I practiced it on my parents, my siblings, my grandparents, uncles, aunts and sundry relatives and could make them do my bidding, Of course, in the beginning, they thought they were bending to my will because of the overflowing love they had for the youngest child in the family. It needed only one piercing glance from my pale green eyes for their hearts and minds to melt.

'I want a cookie, NOW," I would scream. Or it could be 'I want vanilla ice-cream NOW; I want new sneakers NOW; I want a new sport bike NOW; I want a cellphone NOW;' and so on and so on were my commands as I grew up. My parents and other elders in the family happily rushed to comply. School and college followed and my powers of persuasion blossomed into full-scale, subtle attacks on the subconscious of those around me. 'Come on, teacher, give me an A++ in my paper,' and 'Come on professor, give me the best grades in the class' became a routine practice.

In later years, I understood the theory behind the talent I was born with; the ability for 'hypnotic gaze induction'. I could induce a sensuous and soporific effect on any individual of my choosing. It was a celestial gift for me to use, in any way I wish.

Now, the second exhibition of my power was not intentional. I was still recovering from the first one which played out a month earlier. After every episode, my mental energy saps a little, and it takes about three to four weeks before it is restored to an optimum level. I am still working on how to speed up the process.

I was at a big box store in Mississauga, wanting to buy some jute thread for a mixed-arts course I was attending—a combination of craft and oil painting (that is another hobby that I am developing the skills for...)

On the way in, just as I entered the store, a young woman hit me with her shopping cart from behind. Ouch, that hurt, when one of its wheels slammed into my right ankle.

I looked back and the woman, instead of being contrite, began yelling. "Why don't you watch where you are going? Don't you have any sense, dancing in front of customers? Get out of my way."

She was pretty, with the groomed look of an office secretary or personal assistant to an executive and the type who would have several men trying to seduce her. She was wearing a short, yellow skirt and a black blouse with a big white collar. I would have asked her out for coffee on any other day.

"Miss, it wasn't my fault. It was you who hit me from behind."

"I don't care. You were blocking my way... You jumped in front of the cart," she challenged me, her voice rising. "Imbecile."

Other customers were stopping to watch the drama. A young female security guard was approaching us, so I decided to reduce the heat of the situation. I raised my hands and apologized, promising to be more careful.

The young woman walked away in a huff, pushing her trolley along. I waved to the security guard and walked towards another aisle. I was seething with resentment inside, my unforgiving nature not allowing me to let go of the insult.

Me, a top-notch behavioral researcher... And this creature, a nobody, calls me an imbecile in front of so many people?

I crossed a couple of aisles and there she was, in the hardware section, turning around a hammer and balancing it in her left hand.

Closing time neared with only a few customers in the store. She didn't see me approach. I stood behind her and said softly, "Hi, pick up the panel saw as well. Go to aisle number 3 and hit the first person you see on the back of his or her head with the hammer. Then pull the head closer to you and use the saw on the throat. Now."

She turned towards me, her eyes blank and almost opaque. Blinking twice, she rubbed her eyes, smudging her purple mascara. She then picked up a saw from a bottom shelf and walked away, leaving her trolley behind.

I picked up my roll of jute thread and walked to the cash counter. It would take a few minutes for her to reach aisle number 3 at the other end of the store. I went to the parking lot and sat in my car.

Some 20 minutes later, people were running out of the store, and two police cars and an ambulance, with high-pitched sirens blaring and flashing lights, were converging at the store front.

I switched on my car and drove away.

The news flashed on all the TV channels that night and the next morning. The young woman, Sofie-Lou Archam, had attacked an elderly man who was looking for some light bulbs in the superstore. She used a hammer to bash his head in from behind and then sawed through his windpipe, almost decapitating him. The police said there was no connection of any kind between the victim and the assailant. She was crying and screaming while being taken away, saying she heard voices in her head.

It was a messy incident, I learnt later. The man's death was drawn out, causing him unnecessary pain. He bled a lot and the woman was said to be trembling as she tried to slit his throat.

I told myself, 'Never again. I must never use my power in anger or in response to some perceived insult or for personal enjoyment.'

Did I ever feel remorse, or did my conscience react to the incident? It only reinforced my belief that we need to be detached from our actions and I must be cold-blooded and choose only victims who are already feeling suicidal or are outcasts of our society—the unwanted, unloved 'organisms' living on the edges... Of course, the perpetrator and the victim need to be in the same category or wavelength, as you say in today's parlance.

I should tell you about the times I tested my skills on multiple people. It was a partial success. This was at a municipal parking lot in Toronto. A young man had parked his flashy sports car in the lot and walked jauntily into a building without taking a ticket at the pay station. About 30 minutes later, he had come out with a young woman and found a parking enforcement officer placing a ticket on the windshield of his vehicle. I was sitting in my car on the lot, scouting for my guinea pigs, when I heard the loud argument, two rows ahead, which was escalating into an exchange of choice abuses.

I got out of the cart and shouted, "Hey, you!"

They all turned to face me. I snapped my fingers and whispered, urging them to act. "Kick the officer. Punch the man. Strike the woman."

It worked! Three in one go!

A few minutes of mayhem followed. The woman kicked out at the parking officer's groin... He fell to his knees, but got up in an instant and launched himself at the young man. Thrown backwards by the punch, the man coughed and spat out gobs of blood. Recovering soon, he rushed like a bull, swinging his hands; the parking officer ducked, and the fist caught the young woman—in a beautiful upper cut. Her head swung back, as if on springs. A couple of teeth flew from her mouth as she fell screaming on the concrete ground. Two men, who parked their cars, rushed to assist the three while another person called for help on his phone.

I didn't wait to find out the end result. However, I heard later from another parking official the next day that police had charged all three with aggravated assault, although they did not want to file any complaint. Well, not very satisfying, was it? But it reinforced my nagging belief that I can influence others outside the world of riff-raff that I wanted to target! And that I can try for a larger 'audience'.

In another incident—specialists like me call it 'hypnotic coercion'—I persuaded two teenagers to commit a felony.

While strolling down a wide street lined with large maple and oak trees in an upscale neighborhood of Toronto, I saw two youngsters playing with a ball in the middle of the road. As I walked by, they greeted me with a wave and a 'Hi'. Our eyes met, and that was enough.

"Pick a screwdriver from your garages, go to the next street after dusk, walk down the road and scratch the paint of the cars parked by the sidewalks. Target at least ten cars each. Make the scratches as deep as possible. Stab anyone who spots you and approaches you. Puncture the stomach."

The command worked; the young men left long and beautiful streaks on the sides of about 14 cars. However, they did not stab anyone. After a resident yelled at them, they sneaked away into the shadows and disappeared into their homes.

Okay, things were not working the way I wanted it. I need to tweak the method to send effective 'kill' orders to more then one person at a time.

I won't bore you with details of 23 other incidents, including some gory murders and arson, that I planned and executed over the past two years. They worked like a fine-tuned software program—each of them providing a boost in the mastering of my art and the growing power of my reach. I focused on projecting my thoughts and directing my voice commands to individuals and small groups during those exhilarating mind-bending schemes. In addition, there were many gratifying sexual adventures as well—to cool the fires in my inner core. Those fabulous women were all such easy prey!

The other day, while relaxing on my reclining massage chair in front of the television set in my living room, I was quite upset with the news. I felt something changing within me. Channels discussed only inflation, high taxes, the health crisis, encampments in parks, food bank shortages, and general despondency. 'It's time to look at those who control the world,' I said to myself. 'Should I only act against the wretched? Why don't I hit the elites—the politicians, the bureaucrats, and the countless others who vacuum everything into their bloated bellies from the public troughs and the kitchens of the poor?'

Am I developing a conscience? Am I going soft? Wasn't I born to exert my power over every living thing on this earth?

Of course, there was another bit of news that made me sit up and think. Smart officers serve in Toronto, Peel, and other GTA police forces. One of the news readers said cyber specialists were scanning scores of CCTV cameras and other media related to bizarre incidents of violence and deaths, all without any motive. Although I made sure that I hid behind pillars, or behind cars, or wore inconspicuous caps and hats, there were moments when I had to establish eye contact with my 'subjects'. Did any of those cameras capture my face? It must have...

For about a week now, I have been noticing strange cars with tinted windows parked on the road in front of my home. They seem to park at different spots in rotation—the same car appearing every three days or so—and I had seen none of these vehicles before in the small crescent where I live. Are they on a surveillance mission? I might have to lie low and possibly leave the country for the big gambit.

So, watch out for mass protests in the United Kingdom, China, India, Pakistan, France, the Middle East or in Latin American nations; jammed roads and rail networks—with thousands and thousands of people marching for and against inane ideas and ideologies. There will be widespread riots, acts of arson and property destruction. Let anarchy reign. Civil wars rock, right?

First things first, however. Let me now master the last installment of my Advanced Course in Mass Hypnosis, which came to me in a dream sequence over three days and nights a few weeks ago. I was comatose most of the time, after drinking excessive quantities of an ancient and mystical green liquid, with a liquorice-like flavour—you call it Absinthe. I combined it with one of my own creations, a tiny, hallucinogenic pill similar to psilocybin. The slender bottle of green liqueur, with its wormwood twig, matches my pale green eyes.

Do you want to see my eyes? Did you just hear me whisper?

Rejuvenation

The baby whooped in its carriage. Oh, the lights in the mall are so enchanting! The jingling sounds, the rush of people, the vibrant colors, and the enticing scents of cinnamon buns and new clothes make it a magical experience. It's indeed a baby's day out; so much fun. *Chortle, chortle, gurgle, gurgle.* People stop by to peer at the baby covered in swathes of soft, multi-coloured cloth; everybody smiling, nodding and shouting out, "Merry Christmas."

The carriage wheeled around a bend, raced through the corridor to the play area where children were lining up to sit in Santa's lap and get their pictures taken. *Chortle, chortle, gurgle, gurgle.*

On the other side of the mall, a wheel chair crawled.

"Blushhttt," I spat out.

I am not a baby, I am like a baby. True, I wear diapers, but these are adult diapers, and like newborn babies, I have no teeth. I have memories, but I still have many unrealized desires.

I am not in a stroller. My griping, grousing, growling days are gone... those were my young 80s, when I was a mutterer, mumbler and murmurer. Now, I am 92 years old. This is the last scene on my stage, waiting for oblivion ... without teeth, without eyes, without taste, without everything. It's shutting down time!

The Universe has erred. The Universe delayed this... Why? I am an Eternal and the Universe knows it.

"Mb..ly Klitsshmus, Mb..ly Klitsshmus," I mumbled, slouching further, as my caregiver wiped away the drool from my chin.

"Time to go home, Mr. Lindow," she said. "It's already 6:00 pm and time for your pills. My, my, you've wet yourself a lot today... We'll pass the kids' play area and then rush home."

"Bloowty, fluggin blitssh... Vype mi asss, bype byp mi ass."

It was sudden. Something flashed and the baby carriage appeared in front of my wheelchair. Just what I was hoping for... My prayer has been answered... In the nick of time... Salvation! Thank you, Universe!

The baby looked up and our eyes met. An electromagnetic pulse flared and sparkled in an invisible dome that enclosed us.

Our life forces throbbed and changed places. I renewed myself.

I am in the baby carriage, whooping as my mother pushes me across the play area, past the glittering lights of the shop windows, the intoxicating smells of the food court. *Chortle, chortle, gurgle, gurgle...* I know everything. I have seen all this and more before—for over a millennium—and will see many new things in the coming decades and centuries. Life is eternal and effervescent again; with incredible wealth in numbered accounts and vaults in offshore institutions, across the world, to use when I grow up. *Chortle, chortle...*

Oh, the real baby? The baby becometh the man. There he is, slouching in the wheelchair, without teeth, without hearing, drooling, urinating in his diaper. Stupid old man, Lindow... He does not know what happened... He is just a body... Skin and bones. He will not last much longer.

He is now muttering, "Bloowty, shtpid, beeble, puckyoo, pucg."

I make a face at him and spit out, "Yesh, yeesh?" as my mother pushes forward with the stroller into the beguiling and mouth-watering interior of the lingerie shop, one of my favourite places—aha, those pink panties and black, lacy brassieres. Being born again is pure bliss. *Gurgle, gurgle, gulp...*

Acknowledgements

Thanks to fellow writers and friends Mary Ellen Koroscil, Sheila Tucker and Kim Cayer who helped me with the editing of the manuscript and made valuable suggestions for story development.

Also, thanks to:

• All members of the Courtney Park Writers' Group, a strong and supportive organization with several published authors, The Writers' Network (known earlier as the Brampton Writers' Guild), that helps members with top grade critiquing of creative fiction and my wife, Rema, who helped with the proof-reading.

• Reva Leah Stern, for graciously agreeing to write the foreword—and for the generous and sparkling words used to describe the stories in the book.

• David Tucker, for the wonderful blurb for the back cover of the book, and Michael Joll and Konrad Brinck, for their rousing comments about the stories.

• Noted artist Vijay Mohan, for the intriguing cover layout/design.